Elephant Hook

AND OTHER STORIES

Nunatak Fiction

Nunatak is an Inuktitut word meaning "lonely peak"; a rock or mountain rising above ice. During Quaternary glaciation in North America
these peaks stood above the ice sheet and so became refuges for plant
and animal life. Magnificent nunataks, their bases scoured by glaciers,
can be seen along the Highwood Pass in the Alberta Rocky Mountains
and on Ellesmere Island.

Nunatak novels are especially selected works of outstanding fiction by
new western writers. The editors of the Nunatak Fiction series for
NeWest Press are Aritha van Herk and Rudy Wiebe.

Elephant Hook

AND OTHER STORIES

MARTIN SHERMAN

NeWest

First Edition

Canadian Cataloguing in Publication Data

Sherman, Martin, 1953-
  Elephant hook and other stories

  (Nunatak fiction)
  ISBN 0-920897-27-4

  I. Title. II. Series.
PS8587.H47E4 1993   C813'.54   C93-091179-2
PR9199.3.S53E4 1993

Credits:

Cover design: Diane Jensen
Interior design: John Luckhurst/GDL
Editor for the Press: Rudy Wiebe
Financial assistance: NeWest Press gratefully acknowledges the financial assistance of The Alberta Foundation for the Arts, The Canada Council, and The NeWest Institute for Western Canadian Studies.

Printed and bound in Canada by Hignell Printing Limited

NeWest Publishers Limited
Suite 310, 10359 82 Avenue
Edmonton, Alberta T6E 1A9

This is a book of fiction and all characters are fictional.

Some of these stories have been published in various forms prior to this collection: "The Story" in *The Quarterly;* "Baldini Holds the Future in His Hands" in *The Antioch Review;* "Cab Ride" in *The Threepenny Review;* "Laughing Sickness" and "Elephant Hook" in *Canadian Fiction Magazine;* "David and Goliath" in *The New Quarterly;* "You Don't Know" in *NeWest Review;* "Skin Deep" in *Dandelion;* "A Clown's Clown" in *The Hawai'i Review;* "The Sliver" in *Matrix;* "What The Weej Wants" in *Crosscurrents;* "Concentration" and "Walkaround" in *The Calgary Herald.* A slightly different version of "Cab Ride" appeared in *Alberta Re\Bound* (NeWest Press, 1991).

for my parents, for everything

I wish to thank the Alberta Foundation for the Arts for their help in funding me and enabling me to complete this project, and the members of my writers' workshops for their help and advice. Most of all, I thank Linda for her love, her patience, and her belief in me. There would be no words without her.

Contents

Concentration

It's noon. I'm out here on 15th Street with the TV blaring. I'm not doing bad with the volume. There's cars but not too many and I'm sitting on the old trunk right next to the set but the damn sun is washing out the picture no matter how far I crank the contrast up. Alex Trebek I can just tell by his voice, never mind the contestants. Some lady and yesterday's champion, a real estate agent from San Diego. He was too fat yesterday, he's too fat today, I suppose. Some champion. He hits on one match the whole game, a Wild Card and a Take, steals a Mexican vacation and solves "Somewhere Over The Rainbow" which I have seen before. I have seen this one before.

What do you make of that?

This show is called Classic Concentration. Classic. That's supposed to make it okay to use the same phrases they used on the old Concentration show. That was the show for me. They didn't have to spell things out for you.

The prizes they've got on this show. I could use a set of luggage right now looking at mine. I didn't know these bags were wrecked so bad. I mean, we didn't ever go anywhere so how come these bags look like they took the Samsonite test and the monkey won? I could use a new TV, too. This isn't our good one. She kept our good one. But the contrast on that one couldn't do much with this sun either. This is fierce. I could use a drink. And a refrigerator. Not to mention an apartment.

This is the way Wendy wants it, this is the way it's going to be. I'll sit out here and watch my damn show and the hell with the neighbours, the hell with the traffic, the hell with Wendy.

The fat man just missed Home Appliances. Pearl Necklace is behind twenty-one. Twenty-*two* is Home Appliances, and if he matched that with the seven, I could see the puzzle parts behind them. It's seven I really want to see. Seven'll get you going. Never mind. The lady'll have it in a second. Look at her. What'd she expect? She's like crushed when twenty-two flips over and the puzzle part is empty space. Of course twenty-two is empty space, it's seven that's key here. What'd I tell you? That's a can *and* part of a letter. U? You can...lead a horse?

So this, to Wendy, is a waste. Nothing to do with the fact that she can't solve a puzzle worth a damn, I suppose. "What good's it do?" she's always asking. I don't jump on her *religion*, do I? Once, just once, I asked her back, "What good's it do?" So she says, "It gets me through." Well.

Six months ago, Wendy started in on, "You're intelligent. You've got a college degree. If I had a college degree I wouldn't spend my life watching no game shows." And like a fool, like a man walking into an empty elevator shaft, I said, "Any. It's any game shows. And it's just the one." Suddenly, it was, oh, Mr. College Professor, Mr. Perfect English, Mr. Too-smart-for-his-own-wife's-English-but-not-smart-enough-to-get-a-job. And then it was never the same.

Two weeks ago I come back from the Unemployment like always and Wendy doesn't ask me how it went. She just looks at me like something is so damn funny. I say, "What?" but she ignores me. I could hear the sound of one shoe dropping back then.

She was biding her time, I suppose. And this is it, this is old Wendy's finest hour. Well, fine.

That's a man with a scarf around his head. Toothache. U. Can + T. Ache. Got it! "You Can't Take It With You." But the fat man won't see it. Anyway, he's on a roll. Got the pearl necklace for his fat wife, got a riding lawnmower, got some swimwear for his wife and him to take on his Mexican vacation he stole last show. If they make swimwear that big. This is torture. This is the worst. Waiting for the stupids to solve the puzzle.

This is where I scream at the TV and where Wendy says, "They don't care what the puzzle says, Jack. They're going for the *prizes*. They're normal people." Like this is something I have to have explained to me? I could explain things to Wendy but she wouldn't listen. She's got her religion, I've got my show. And whose is better? When Jackson died, it wasn't me who asked, "How can God let this happen? What did I ever do to deserve this, Jack? He was just a baby." She was helping me put his things away. We thought, someday, there might be another baby. She was holding his shoes which he'd worn exactly once. And when I held her, holding those shoes, and I said, "Shhh," and she cried and cursed God, you could've taken a picture and it would have been Couple Whose Baby Died without even needing the caption.

The fat man finally got it. Alex Trebek is walking over to the board to explain to people even stupider than the fat man how he solved the puzzle. His fat wife is cheering for him somewhere in the audience, thinking what a genius she married. What a prize.

The next part I could do in my sleep. You get X number of seconds and try to remember what cars are where on the board, then match all the cars. Big deal for me. I've got a photographic memory. This is how I got through college with the A's and how I got through work and got promoted until they found out a computer could do everything I did. Only a hundred times faster. Big deal for me.

This is something I never lorded over Wendy. Wendy's real sensitive about her education even though she's ten times as smart as me. Wendy takes trash and makes beautiful things out of it. Used to. Used to sell things at swap meets, things she made out of trash. Don Quixote on his horse made out of old cans and rusty metal. This three-foot tree made out of barbed wire fencing left over from her Dad's farm with must have been twenty rusty wire kids playing in the branches. She started getting calls to go to this or that craft show. Got *commissioned* to do pieces for lobbies. Now she's got a show at The Women's Gallery. Only no more Don Quixote, no more kids. Now she takes the beautiful things she's made and turns them back to trash.

Commercial over. New contestant. Housewife from Iowa. This is the home contestant portion where people at home send in their puzzles and, if you get yours picked, the winner plays the championship car matching game for both of you. Usually, the puzzles are pretty lame.

This housewife is sharp. She knows where to pick the squares, where the puzzle parts give the most information. Some numbskulls will even go for the corners, not her. And lucky? First, she misses. Then, he misses. Then, she hits a Give card and matches it to the one he turned so she doesn't have to give him a thing and still gets two puzzle pieces. Not much there. Two sticks on different parts of the board. Could be a bat, a rolling pin, a propeller, anything. Then she hits two more in a row. One matches the Cosmetics card she turned over on her first try and then two Patio Furnitures out of the blue. It's a bat and an oar. And there's part of a car. Batter late than never? For batter or worse? No.

This is the beauty of it, sifting through all the possible answers. This is the real challenge for me. Knowing everything's there, not leaving out a single clue because they must all mean something. Okay, sure, there's a bat and a boat in the puzzle and they're not really part of the answer but that's what makes the stick an oar and the ballplayer a batter. You've got to have those other parts but the trick is to focus on what's part of the answer and know what it's called. The oar, for instance, could be a paddle but it's in a rowboat not a canoe. You see what I mean?

This is what I could never explain to Wendy. I used to go to church with her and when I stopped it wasn't because I stopped believing in God. I never believed in God. Just that there was some purpose, some kind of meaning to life. The sin, the salvation, angels, heaven and hell, all that stuff was just ornaments. Like God. It's wondering about the meaning of it all that makes people go to church. When you get there, that's when they distract you with all the other crap. Like, if there's a message, there must be a Message-Maker and He's got to be the most powerful force in the universe and this is what He wants you to do. God's Plan. So when Wendy asks the preacher why Jackson had to die all she gets is, "We mustn't question God's Plan." Well, that's why you showed up in church in the first place, right?

The housewife solves it. I get it about the same time but, even though

I pride myself on my speed, I suddenly realize that's not the point. Not for me, it isn't.

Now Alex Trebek walks over and tells everyone what the clues spell out. The batter is really a hitter and it's the *motion* of the oar that's the clue. The car's hoisted up on a jack. Get it? Hitter, row, jack. "Hit The Road, Jack."

Then I'm just sitting there laughing and, with the cars going by and me howling away, I can barely hear Alex Trebek announce that the puzzle was sent in by Wendy Sullivan, my own sweet wife. Of course, I already figured this out.

They must have notified her a couple weeks back and she's just been waiting for today. And this, the bags on the sidewalk, the old TV, the new locks on the doors, the TV puzzle just for me, this is the other shoe dropping. I look up at the big front window in our house and sure enough, Wendy's peeking out at me from behind the blinds. Well, I'm laughing, Wendy. Laughing, see? It's funny. Some things still are funny. I hope you win your damn car.

What I don't like is that she really thinks I need to have this explained to me on TV. Like unless I see it on "Concentration" this wouldn't sink in. This is the difference between her religion and the way I think. To me, everything you ever do, or see, or think about, is some kind of a clue to the puzzle which you've got to figure out. But I'm going to figure it out for myself. I'm not going around knowing that there's an answer out there and then not looking for it. Wendy won't even bother. The only faith she's got is faith in God and none in me.

So I'm sitting here in the bright sun, with all my stuff in bags, and I've got all the clues in the world. Every little thing I've done in my life running through my photographic memory. Pictures of me as a kid with all my little awards, Wendy and me and two strangers as witnesses at our wedding, the birth, me taking my mouth off of Jackson's dead mouth screaming at Wendy, "Do something, you moron. Do something." And I haven't got the least idea what it all means.

Where the hell is Alex Trebek when you really need him?

Walkaround

Behold the Mighty Marcus: slipping the toga over my head, knotting the cord around my waist, checking the winged silver helmet I will wear.

In the walkaround I am a miserable Mercury, dissolute, stout, and tramp-faced. Behind me, the younger clowns scramble for their props. They swear and sweat into their walkaround costumes, regaining breath after an acrobatic act from which I, fat and fifty, am pardoned. They wish it was already over, this walkaround, this chore, the sooner the better. A walkaround, after all, is filler—a quick visual gag whose sole purpose is to allow the trapeze act enough time to assemble its rigging. Put on the costume, grab the props, dash for the entrance before the Bulgarian trick riders finish their act. Then we'll spill out from backstage, loop once around the hippodrome track, just long enough for the ringstock to shovel up the remnants of the horse act before the flyers come on. As we circle, the audience follows us, distracted from the flurry of the men with shovels. Then their eyes drift back to the rings, to the heart of the circus.

I repair my props. They give way to rot like the rest of us and I sit in this huddle of blue steamer trunks between acts stemming the flow of time and decay. The silver boots rest upon my drawn-up knees. Hunched forward, I hold my eye to a jeweler's glass, delicately wielding a surgical scalpel, etching a personal history of pain into the leather. The gypsy music, the hoofbeats, the noises of fear from the crowd as the Bulgarians leap on and off the Clydesdales form a familiar rhythm to me, like my own tired breath—a rising, a fracture of lung, a slow sigh. The fire music starts as, in each ring, the riders, standing on horseback, juggling torches, prepare to leap through flaming hoops. Three minutes 'til walkaround.

Julia sits front and centre, a few yards from the hippodrome track. She sits erect, unblinking, her Texas summer sky eyes dismissing the whirling fire torches of the Bulgarian riders, oblivious to the overhead flash of spotlight on the aerialists' sequins. She awaits my entrance. Julia knows how to look past the distractions, past style to substance.

In her first two years on the show, Julia's eyes never fixed on mine though I contrived to put myself in front of her at every chance. I did not see their colour then as the warm Texas summer but rather as the bitter heart of a fissured glacier.

Julia's eyes will track my motion around the rings, sliding from left to right as I appear and disappear. She sits there alone with such palpable purpose that no curious child dares approach to offer her his stale, choking popcorn. She sits there with such dignity. Such beauty.

The music is obscured for a moment by the inane chatter of the younger clowns. I used to be one of them—a young, athletic white-face, a joey, the clown of supreme control, master of the fool augustes, disdainful of the tramp. But then we all used to be joeys. Only the stumblebums and self-admitted failures would consent to be the fool auguste.

There is an unwritten circus caste system headed by the Brahmins of the trapeze descending through the lion-tamers, acrobats, showgirls, to the bottom—to the Untouchable clowns. Clown alley, the array of circus trunks that designates our dressing room, is inevitably placed behind the horse stables.

We clowns have our own divisions—the white-face, the grotesque flesh-faced auguste, and the tramp. I was once the white-face King of Clowns—my advice was sought by other clowns, new clowns imitated my walk and my expressions, clowns from other shows spent days-off at our circus to see me work. My make-up was clean, delicate; my motions, a swift smooth flow of style and grace. My juggling and acrobatics defied all laws of gravity and motion.

Joeys are a rarity now among the sea of orange-flesh auguste clown faces. And I am the sole tramp clown. Waiting in the dung-heavy air for the walkaround.

I had a solo juggling act in my white-face days. I preceded the lion act—a pathetic gladitorial re-enactment, Hercules and the Seven Scourges of Rome. I was just a coverage act while the ringstock wheeled in the cages, but there, for those moments, I stood alone before the crowd, demanding their attention, promising them miracles. The three silver balls, framed in the spotlight, whirled in constantly shifting patterns, floating in mid-air independent of my hands. The audience sat silently watching the designs transform, as though huddled around the licking hypnotic flames of a campfire.

When the lion act was ready, a solitary trumpet salute signalled me and I would look behind me, noticing the lions for the first time. In mock fear, I would fling the balls up in the air and leap away, grabbing for protection the gladiator net Hercules kept beside the cage. As I held it out to ward off the beasts, the juggling balls would land in the mesh to my apparent astonishment. I would take my bows and leave. The applause was, at first, merely polite. The more I exhibited the act, the deeper I became absorbed in my performance until the world outside became mere distraction, an annoyance. The applause began to grow louder, lengthen, until even the band had to wait before launching into the lion-tamer's music, the theme from *Ben Hur*.

The peroxided, toothy Hercules complained. Marcus the Measly worked too close to his animals. Marcus the Minute endangered the life of the Mighty Hercules. Marcus the Miniscule was ruining years of training invested in the Seven Scourges. My act frightened them, he whined. The flash of the silvery balls upset them, made them wild and uncontrollable. The truth, I said, was that the motion of the balls helped mesmerize the lions into the near-comatose state Hercules required of them in performance. Audience members, I said, achieved the same condition simply by watching his act.

The next day, as if by accident, I rolled a ball under the cage and into the centre of the ring. I unlatched the cage, walked in like Daniel, oblivious to the circle of beasts, bent and picked up the stray ball. Only after latching the cage door behind me did I pretend to notice the lions and faint.

It was as though, simply by stepping out of my ring and into the lion cage, I had somehow shattered the natural order of circus hierarchy and blundered into the world of the performers.

Soon, I think, these bright flowers of greasepaint that wave in the entrance ramp will wilt with age. Only the most arrogant will survive the years, only the leather-hearted will not rot or turn to dust. Clown Alley will be ravaged with time, leaving a mere handful of us, dried flowers. We will create of ourselves an arrangement, together mount an exhibition, we survivors, eternal and recurring—The Three Rings of Hell. Laaaaaaaadies and Gentlemen, Mortals and Olympians, behold.

And Julia will behold.

The boots I am carving are crushed, toeless army boots, soleless, ruined. The silver spray paint is heavily cracked and peeling along the sides. I carefully connect the boots to the nearly invisible wires that dangle from a harness I'll wear around my shoulders. Seen from a few feet back, the boots seem to float in front of me, just out of arm's reach. The white foam-rubber wings glued to the boots' ankles are so fragile that they flutter and beat with every movement, every breath of wind, giving them the appearance of flight. I put down the boots and pick up the giant foam rubber feet I'll wear in the walkaround.

Two minutes.

I served a week's suspension for entering the lion cage. My cherished juggling solo was cut but, backstage, the performers began to talk to me. Even Julia seemed changed—I would catch moments when her icy gaze focused on me. Moments, as her eyes met mine and lifted past me, when the look on her face displayed a strange combination of memory and curiosity.

Performers never watched the show but everyone claimed to have seen me. I felt, in that week, nothing but scorn for them. I was, I believed, learning something true and eternal about the nature of spectacle. I recognized what the performers never could—the nature of the audience appetite, the sinister glint of saliva in a child's mouth.

And it seemed the more I displayed my disdain for their company, the more eagerly the performers sought out mine. I began to get suggestions from them as to how I might stumble into their acts.

My part in the show expanded gradually, showing up, as if by accident, in a growing number of acts until at last I was performing one long act of my own throughout the show.

Early in the circus, when the solo trapeze artists appeared, I awaited Julia's entrance, displaying a desperate and incurable love for her, watching her every motion, mesmerized by every gesture, cheerleading the crowd for her. At the conclusion of her act, I rushed to her and drew from my coat pocket a tattered rose which immediately lost its petals and crumbled in my hands. Mortified and desolate, I retreated to a spot just outside the rings and began to create a little garden patch which I raked and hoed energetically until it met my exacting standards. From the pockets of my costume, I pulled out a large seed and carefully planted it, erecting alongside the spot a large picture of a perfect Lincoln rose. I watered the seed and waited next to the garden, impatiently tapping my foot, whistling, pacing back and forth, nervously checking the empty spot. With a sudden inspiration I hurried from the arena.

I returned during the elephant act, clutching a large bag marked "Fertilizer." I inverted the bag over the garden but found to my dismay that it was empty. Then I saw the elephants. I wandered toward the rings, watched as a ringstock ran to scoop a pile of freshly-dropped manure from the track. I grinned and stepped up to the hindquarters of the nearest elephant, held the empty bag under its tail. Nothing. I pumped the tail up and down. Nothing. I angrily shoved the tail aside and the elephant responded, swinging her tail back into my face. I tottered about unsteadily as though reeling from the blow, and at last fell onto my rump. I sat suddenly erect, sniffing the air, my face slowly contorting in disgust. I rose slowly, with enforced dignity, turned and stared down at the apparent source of my discomfort. As the elephant act finished, I walked stiffly from the arena, delicately tugging the rear of my costume away from my bottom.

The next act began with a blackout: a single spotlight illuminated a man in a pair of silver-sequined bathing trunks. The spot followed as he climbed a rope-ladder to a high perch. Drum roll. A second spotlight focused on a small tank of water on the ground and there I was, clad only in longjohns, happily washing my soiled costume in the water. As the laughter died down, I was dragged from the arena by two beefy ring attendants.

I reappeared during the wire-walking act. While the act went on I climbed up to the wire, arriving just before the Caspiri Brothers were about to attempt the Dive of Death. Gino, on the far side of the wire, was to dive over his brother, Emilio, somersault through the air and land on the wire. While Emilio chalked his shoes, I reached the perch and walked past him backwards onto the wire, still dressed in my longjohns, holding my dripping costume. I neared the centre of the wire, kneeled and began hanging my laundry on the wire to dry. The brothers shouted at me to get off while I waved angrily at them to leave me alone. They came after me, Emilio in front and Gino behind. My legs shook in mock fear and the wire shivered. I snatched up my costume, swaying with each motion, and started slowly to back away, sliding toe to heel, until I bumped into Gino. I reached behind me, blindly discovering him, patting his knees, thighs, my hand slapped as it neared his buttocks. I twisted my head and Gino smiled savagely. I ran, tiptoed, to the centre of the wire. The brothers moved in. Emilio grabbed at me as Gino leapt, flipping completely over both me and his brother, while I dropped from the wire holding my costume like a pathetic parachute over my head, landing safely in a hidden net below.

I walked sadly over to my empty garden, ignoring the ovation, climbed into my wet costume, and sat on the ring curb.

Julia came on next, this time with a flying trapeze troupe. Again, I watched her every move longingly, tearfully, dabbing at my eyes with the corner of my sleeve. As the act finished, I rose to applaud her. I wrung out a stream of tears from my sleeve over the garden plot and from the mound of dirt a huge red rose burst into bloom. As the aerialists took their bows, I plucked the flower and ran with it to her. She took it, gently kissed my forehead and we left the arena arm in arm.

Suddenly, I was a star. When we played New York, my performance was singled out for a rave review in *The New York Times*. The show began to feature me in posters and in the circus program. And Julia, I was certain, was beginning to fall in love with me.

My problem was Raul, Julia's "catcher" in the flying trap act. Twice a day she flung herself blindly through the air, twisting, flipping with her fingers outstretched in perfect faith that his strong wrists and massive hands would wrench her from limbo and return her in precise rhythm to her own trapeze. It was not a leap of faith—merely the articulation of their relationship.

Julia in the air was a creature divorced from the rest of humanity, leaden with its burden of gravity. The trapeze bar seemed merely a prop to convince people she couldn't really stay aloft on her own.

Julia was a rarity—a flyer who worked both solo trapeze and with a flying trapeze troupe. Though only solo trap acts work without a net, the acts the audience remembers are the flyers. The nature of the flying act—the constant hunt for greater power in the swing, an ever-later release, a supreme height, for the narcotic bliss of those weightless seconds—overshadows the complex delicacy of balance in the solo act and the flying stars radiate that hunger for one more twist, one more flip. But there was nothing of that in Julia. Even as she pumped forward toward the triple somersault, her face retained an emptiness. There was no guttural grunt as she folded her body into a spinning blur. And when she uncoiled into the slap of flesh, Raul's massive hands sliding over her forearms, clenching her wrists, Julia was impassive, expressionless, almost mechanical. She smiled only when she posed, arms outstretched, to accept the crowd's applause. And when she watched me.

I *had* surprised her that first time. When she finished her solo act, bowed and flashed her mechanical smile, I was suddenly there before her holding the naked rose as its petals dissolved from the stem. There was shock in her face, as though I was some madman intent on rape, then relief as I lowered my head to watch the petals waft through the air and onto the ground. Before I turned away in despair, I would raise my eyes for a single glance and see her smile. After the flying act, when I presented her with the rose in full bloom, I expected the smile again. Shock undoubtedly showed on my face as she kissed my forehead and walked off arm in arm with me. Backstage, that first time, I grabbed her and yelled, "You were incredible!" She shook herself free, handed me the rose and said, "Raul is going to kill you."

Raul arrived a moment later with just that in mind but he never caught me. When three muscular Bulgarians at last managed to restrain him, he was turning over one huge wardrobe box after another as I leaped across their tops. Minutes later we sat in the owner's office; Raul, still glowering, and me, with a contrived look of repentance. I was sorry, I said. It was merely that I felt compelled to approach Julia again, I explained, as though the audience was forcing me to win her affections. Exactly right, agreed the owner, and not only was I right in what I did, I was going to keep right on doing it every performance. He insisted, despite my protestations and despite Raul's violent departure from the office. And the act was a sensation.

The oversized feet are sculpted with thick knots of muscle and heavy root-like veins—not at all the graceful feet one might expect of the god of messengers. I carved them from blocks of foam rubber with an electric knife, smoothed and detailed them with a series of progressively smaller shears until the foam resembled the delicately pebbled texture of human skin. The lower edges are black with dirt and the ashes of a thousand cigarettes crushed before entering the arena. The heels of both feet are hardened and eroded; the painted toenails are chipped. Three years ago, the big toe of the right foot was amputated by a sadistic youngster who trod upon it viciously and was so delighted with the pain I feigned that he ground his little foot into the track, ripping the foam. I replaced the toe with a little foam rubber pun—a tiny ear of corn rising from the foot in a bright green shock. I crush the spongy surface, wringing out the remnants of every other walkaround.

One minute.

Julia never talked to me off-stage. Every moment of her free time was jealously guarded by Raul. But during the walk-off, after she took my arm, we began to talk. In those moments I would question her: who was she, where had she come from. Through her fixed smile she whispered her story to me.

Raul discovered her in a west Texas high school gymnastics meet while on a three day break from the Hagenback-Wallace Circus. He was thirty-three, becoming too thickly muscular to contort himself fluidly through the air. His older brother could no longer be relied on to catch him every time. Their contract for next year had not been renewed. Day one of the break he had spent wandering the bars of El Paso. He woke up dry mouthed and lost in a neighbouring town and wandered into the open doors of the high school gym to use the bathroom. He watched Julia sweep every event in the competition. She was sixteen.

Raul seemed like a god to her, a swarthy, powerful, fiery god who looked at her from another dimension. In his eyes the high school gymnast was already a memory, something that had been there before he began to create her. She left with him before the awards presentation. He taught her how to walk, how to smile, how to cook and sew and make love to him. And he taught her how to fly.

He's an old man, he's a fool. He knows nothing about what he does except trivia. Leave him.

She laughed, "What? And be a fat El Paso housewife picking up after three kids?"

Is that so bad?

"Yes," she hissed. "Raul doesn't own me. We're not married and when I want to leave I will. When I'm ready. When my act is perfect. Shhh, here's Raul."

There will always be Raul.

"No."

You may fly between the bars thinking it's your act but you will always throw your hands out to be caught. He will always be there.

"I've got the solo act."

*Solo? During your **solo** act there are trap acts going on in all three rings. It isn't a feature. Come with me. I got an offer from Monaco. The Royal Circus. My own terms. I can give you a feature. We can leave next week.*

"I didn't get an offer."

They want me and I want you.

"Because without me where is the sweet little ending to *your* act. You need me."

I don't need you, Julia. Don't you see that? I want you and you want...

"I've got what I want."

Come away with me. Let's leave this sick palace.

"Leave? I love this. The way they look at us. For a few hours we take their cares away and make them happy."

You're wrong. They hate Raul and the rest of the performers.

"What about me? They love me."

Without me, they would hate you, too.

"You? You think you do that?"

Listen to me. It was the Romans who created circuses, Julia. Fashioned acrobats after their beautiful and distant gods. The Roman gods have disappeared, debased and humiliated, laughed at, in the legends the Romans created.

That's what you are to them, Julia. Beautiful, distant, perfect. They want to crush you, to watch you fail. Every time you succeed, every trick you perform to perfection, makes them hate you more. It's me they love,

the bumbling fool, the little Jesus crucified in my every step. They see
themselves in me. When I go back with that rose, when you take it from
me and kiss me, I'm taking you out of the clouds and making you real.
Without me you are nothing to them. Come away with me. You can never
make them happy.

Julia stopped. We were near the end of our walk-off. She looked
over at me and then back toward Raul waiting at the curtain flaps. She
tugged at my arm and continued walking, whispering between the fixed
lips of her stage smile, "I can make them happy."

Twenty years ago, Merv Griffin asked me what I thought I'd be doing
in twenty years. I was the darling of the press back then. I worked
advance, arriving two days ahead of the first performance to publicize
the show—a natural newspaper feature, doing talk shows, variety
shows, pumping the gate.

Merv was in his mod phase; big collars, flower ties, wide belt on his
still-trim tummy, his trouser hems clanging like church bells on his
ankles. Merv wore a neat little beard—an invitation for his guests to
join him in self-mockery. The audience loved each little fur-face jibe.
Merv insisted that I put on my make-up in front of his studio audience
so I arrived in street clothes. He announced only my name. I walked
onto the set, tripped over the microphone cord, clutched wildly at the
falling mike stand, wrapping the cord around my ankles, stumbled over
the step to the stage set, and crashed through Merv's mock-up desk,
completely flattening it. There was stunned silence, only Merv and his
crew clapping and laughing. Merv pulled out a full-face poster of me
in make-up announcing my clown identity. I bowed to the enthusiastic
and embarrassed applause. As I transformed myself at the make-up
table from an invisibly familiar "bright, articulate young man" to my
celebrated white-faced alter ego, Merv questioned me. Why I did it,
where I learned, when I joined. . . .

"What do you think you'll be doing in twenty years?"

I didn't say, "Rising each morning to the ahhh-whish of my true
love's ventilation, suctioning phlegm from my true love's throat,

dumping the urine from my true love's bag, sponging her, dressing her, baby-fooding breakfast to her. Wheeling her to see me in her every waking hour."

"Twenty years?" is what I said. "Probably be growing a beard."

Perhaps memory has a way of layering meaning into history or maybe there was really something different about her solo act that night. All the same twists and turns, the balancing and the last-second regaining of equilibrium suddenly seemed infused with purpose. I'd watched her solo act a thousand times, each performance a perfect replica of the last. Julia was utterly absorbed in the act—as though the audience was peeping through a keyhole at a private ritual, as though the world below had ceased to exist.

Halfway through the act, Julia would stand on the bar, pumping the single trapeze into motion. On the swinging trap she did a series of simple tricks: a giant swing, a dislocate, a bird cage. They had always seemed almost careless gestures, a kid on a park swing, no more challenging for her than balancing on the still bar. This time there was a ferocity to the motion, her fingers clenched on the guy wires, the muscles on her legs and arms prominent with the strain, her small body wrenching with undulation. Each swing seemed more violent, danger-ous, each trick seemed to intensify the audience's hunger for more and after every trick she pumped the swing again until the trapeze arced to the horizontal. She pulled herself upright on the bar for her finale and for the first time acknowledged the audience. Julia hung on casually with her right hand and with her left made giant sweeping motions over the crowd. She held a single finger aloft and the crowd chanted, "One!" Swing. "Two!" Swing. She arched forward into "Three!" I watched her launch herself into space. In memory I can still see the moment Julia looked down into the faces of the crowd staring up at her, waiting for her to perform her miracle and catch herself by the heels. In memory, she is still frozen there, smiling again and waiting to hear something that never sounds.

I adjust my toga over the harness that holds the silver boots. The harness is strapped to my chest and a strong thin flexible wire sprouts out from the harness through the toga. The boots dangle from the end of the wire, appearing to float in mid-air, inches from my outstretched fingers. When I grasp at them, the tiny wings on their sides seem to flutter.

I put on the winged cap, completing my transformation to a tramp-faced Mercury. His flying shoes have somehow escaped, condemning him to chase them futilely in swollen, earthbound feet. I take an experimental step forward, feel the spring in my legs. By the time I return my legs will be leaden, weighed down with the burden of her witness.

One day we will fill these rings with acts of quotidian purgatory— a man who shaves continuously, his beard growing faster than his hand can shear; a mother and her child who pursue each other around the ring, stacking and strewing toys; a gardener watering his rows of thirsting flowers with a thimble-sized can. I will circle them in walkaround, reaching in vain for my escaping shoes, the sounds of my gasping lungs in harmony with Julia's mechanized ventilation, passing eternally before the unblinking, drying eyes of my love.

The music rises. There is the collective sigh from the crowd as the Bulgarians successfully complete their somersaults through rings of fire. The sound of applause mingles with the pounding hoofbeats of the Clydesdales leaving the ring. The band switches from gypsy music to the clown theme. As we go out, I hear the applause die down.

And then the laughs.

Baldini Holds the Future in His Hands

Baldini warned me, don't meet the first doctor. The first doctor you meet is Death. I said, I always thought it was the last. Oh, no, said Baldini, by that time it's already too late.

Baldini is as good as dead.

The first doctor didn't say anything about dying. He said it was a baby. That was good news. He was the only one who had any good news. The rest they sent us to just turned it all to dust. The second doctor said, this baby doesn't move too much. Hell, I said, Sheila told you that. That's why we're here. He smeared jelly all over her belly and put the microphone on her and let us watch the TV. Stuff moved but it wasn't the baby, it was Sheila. All that stuff in there. I guess they know what's baby and what's not. I said, how come its head looks like a pear? Oh, they all do, the second doctor said. Sheila said she wasn't worried. If you're not worried, I said, why the hell do you have jelly on your belly? Sheila said, shhh.

The third doctor we got sent to said we have a problem. You mean Sheila and me, I said, or you too? We're all in this together, he said. Now Sheila was worried. He said, hydrocephalus. Sheila just squeezed my hand. Well just what is that, I said. And the doctor said, there's water on the brain. Oh, no. That's what we said.

The fourth doctor said, do you want this baby? This one, I said, is this baby going to live? We don't know, he said, but if it does it probably won't be normal. Like normal what, I said, like normal retarded or like a vegetable? Like a vegetable, said the doctor.

Sheila and I talked about it. We didn't want this baby, I didn't for sure. Sheila said she didn't. Sheila wanted to know about other babies. Are they all going to have water on the brain, she said. The fourth doctor said, oh, no. That hardly ever happens. I said, why did it happen to this one? We don't know, said the doctor, I'm sorry. Well, if we don't want this baby what happens? Sheila wanted to know. This isn't an abortion, said the fourth doctor. I don't want an abortion, Sheila said. This isn't one, the doctor said, you're too far along for that. We just deliver the baby now. You can hold the baby. If you want, we can have the baby baptized. Oh God, was all Sheila could say. Shhh, I told Sheila.

The fifth doctor said we couldn't do it. It was a lady doctor. She was younger and prettier than Sheila. She was pregnant, too. What do you mean we can't do it, I said, he just said we can. His concern is your wife, the fifth doctor said. My job is to take care of the baby. My baby is going to die, said Sheila. We don't know that, said the fifth doctor. We need more information. We need to do some tests. I said, it has water on the brain. Sometimes there are things we can do, operations, the fifth doctor said. This baby's going to be a vegetable, I said. We don't know that, the lady doctor said.

She showed us pictures, the fifth doctor. Hydrocephalics. They have giant bald pear heads. They look like men of the future from a Superman comic book. In the comics, they need giant heads to hold their super-intelligent brains. But real ones are retarded or vegetables or dead.

The fourth doctor told us we couldn't have the baby in this hospital. We had to move to another hospital to get away from the fifth doctor, he said, because once the baby's born it's out of my hands. So we did.

They gave Sheila a shot and we just had to wait. Then she started to have contractions. Sheila screamed and screamed and I held her hand and said, breathe, and wiped her forehead like we did in class. Like this was just what we learned in class. Then the baby was born, all bloody, and they washed it and gave it to Sheila. A girl. Sheila cried and held the baby and I held Sheila and we waited but the baby didn't die. All she did was breathe.

They took the baby away. The baby wasn't going to die. They took the baby away and told us that they had to bring it back to the first hospital. One of the doctors, I didn't know which any more, told us that.

The fifth doctor, the pregnant one, took care of our baby. She talked to Sheila. She said, it's no good. There's nothing that an operation can do. Sheila said, let my baby die. Please, let my baby die. We can't, the fifth doctor said, it's against the law. Why can't you just unhook her, I said, just unhook her and see what happens. We can't, the doctor said, I'm sorry.

The baby was in a transparent plastic bed. There were tubes coming out everywhere. There were three machines hooked up to her. One to breathe for her. One to exchange her blood for somebody else's. One to tell us she was alive. She had a big bald pear head. She was just lying there. The future.

I was talking to Baldini. He was dying. Doctors wouldn't touch him without masks and gloves.

What's it like, I said.

Like a giant Get Out Of Jail Free card, said Baldini. When they told me, it was like I could hear the cell door unlock.

It's not right, I said. This baby *wants* to die but they won't let it. Why can't they just unhook her and let her die, I said.

I hear you, Baldini said.

That doctor will have a normal baby.

I know, Baldini said.

What am I going to do, I said.

Let me take care of it, said Baldini. I got nothing to lose.

Elephant Hook

It was me that showed Donna how to ride the elephants. It's a little like water-skiing. You stand on their shoulders and pull back on the bridle ropes hooked on the headdress. There's a little trick to staying smooth. You've got to just relax your legs like shock absorbers because their shoulders roll up under you whenever they walk. It's not hard once you've had a little practice.

Donna did fine. She's got great balance and real strong legs. She used to be a gymnast—she's got one of those acrobat bodies, real strong in the arms and back and legs. A bit short and thick for show dancing but unless she was standing next to Kathy, who has like the ultimate showgirl body, nobody can tell in those huge arenas we played.

She may not have looked it but Donna was probably the best dancer of any of us. Okay, it's just dancing in a circus but, out of fifteen showgirls, there are some girls who've been in lots of musicals. A couple have even been on Broadway. Chorus line, but still….

Donna's big problem was she was too good. She just loved to dance and once she got going something clicked on in her. We were always having to remind her to tone it down, for God's sake, or people wouldn't look at the acts. She'd listen for a few days and then forget. It wasn't her fault.

The other thing about Donna is how she wasn't afraid of the elephants. Not that she should have been though most new girls are. I can't really blame them—you'd think something that big would always be knocking people over or stepping on their toes but an elephant knows exactly where everybody is all the time. Still, the first time you see one of the old girls up close from the front she's a pretty alarming sight. Her legs are like old grey trees with big knotty knees and her trunk—I mean you know it's her nose but still—it looks like nothing you've ever seen before, this unbelievably powerful tube of muscle snaking down at you. Kathy says it looks like what half the men she's ever dated think *they* look like. Anyway, to see her trunk come down can be really frightening if you're not used to it. Her nostril's always snuffling, like a wet pink-and-black vacuum cleaner, touching you all over with her "thumb"—that's what they call the tip of her trunk.

The tip does look like a kind of finger and she picks up everything with it but it's also like another set of eyes for her—elephants have pretty bad eyesight—so she explores everything with her "thumb" like a blind person, kind of a quick brushing, petting motion. Most of the new girls jump out of their skins the first time they feel that touch. Actually, Donna and me are about the only people I know who weren't scared. It's people's touches that scare me.

When India, that's my elephant, the one I ride, when India pats me, it reminds me of junior high—the way my girlfriends and I used to talk, just now and then touching each other's shoulders or elbows, and the feeling of the fingertips is like you've just gotten a little gift.

Junior high! That was a long time ago, longer than I care to remember. Then, all of a sudden, when you're in high school you don't touch anymore—it's sick or something. And all of the touching comes from boys, which is something else entirely—not giving, more like taking something away. After a while, you kind of forget about that other kind of touch.

When Sudesh, that's Donna's elephant, reached down with her trunk Donna wasn't scared. She put out her hands, palms up and let Sudesh snuffle. Kathy said it was just that Donna's too stupid to know better. But it wasn't that. She was like me. She liked them.

Showgirls only ride elephants during "menage," which is short for menagerie. It's supposed to be this big production number with all sorts of exotic animals like llamas and ostriches and chimps and clowns, but they're all just too crazy so all they use are elephants and showgirls.

Anyway, you don't ride them for very long. Just down the back track and into the centre ring. Then they kneel down and you climb over their heads and run about halfway down their trunks before you jump. Then we style and hold that pose while the elephants do their tricks. My big part comes next where I lie down and India lifts her right foreleg and puts it about six inches over my face and holds it there. It looks scary but like I said, she knows exactly where I am and would never hurt me. Then we style again and pirouette down the back track.

It's actually a really good part because the other girls have to stay out through the whole menage number which must go on for another five minutes while Donna and me are already in the dressing room.

After we finish menage in St. Petersburg, Donna says to me, "Who's my elephant trainer?" Which isn't right because he's only a ringstock. He just leads them out for all the production numbers. But I know who she's talking about.

"His name is Jared."

"Does he have a girlfriend?"

We're peeling off our menage leotards in the dressing room. It's not a real dressing room, just a group of steamer trunks surrounded by big blue screens.

I say, "Jared? I don't think so. He's new."

"He's gorgeous," says Donna.

I don't say anything, just start fixing my face. I'm thinking, she's right. He's got a big, tanned, muscled body, and pale green eyes that are scary the way he seems to look inside of you. But anybody can tell his long blond hair is straight out of a bottle. His name sounds phony, too. I don't really care. Everybody but me seems to have dyed their hair and changed their names. Kathy says that probably half the criminals in the world hide out in the circus and anyone in the show who hasn't committed a crime is busy planning one. The bad thing about all the dyed hair is I'm a natural redhead and all the guys I meet just seem interested in finding out if I'm really red "down there."

Donna stands behind me and brushes her hair. She's got nice thick, straight black hair. "So? Is he nice?"

"How should I know?" I say. "He's new, like I said, and I've hardly said a word to him."

"I think he's nice. I don't think he ever uses his hook on the elephants." I'm sort of surprised to hear that from Donna, that she noticed about the hooks.

The ringstocks have these sticks with a little metal hook on the end that they can snag behind the elephants' ears or worse, through a hole in ear. The ear's about the only part of them that's really sensitive. You can beat them nine ways with a stick anywhere else on their bodies and they hardly bat a lash but one little hook in the ear and they heel like a puppy. Nobody uses the hook much when Karl, that's the real trainer, is around 'cause he'll go off like a cannon. Anyway, just showing the hook will bring them in line. But some of the guys'll hook the elephants as soon as Karl's out of sight. They must think it makes them big men to lead a mountain of muscle around with one flick of the wrist. So when she says that, I think, maybe I'm wrong, maybe Jared is nice.

Donna sits herself down at her trunk next to mine. She pops up her mirror and goes to work with lip-liner. Then she stops and starts to giggle.

"What's so funny?" I ask her.

"He likes my butt. He says from behind when I'm riding on Sudesh my cheeks roll like ocean waves. Just like that, like ocean waves."

And then I know he's a phony because that's what he said to me in Winter Quarters. But I don't tell Donna.

Donna started hanging out with Kewpie and me. Kewpie is really Q.P., short for Queer Purser John. He's the train purser, which means he basically runs all the business on the circus train where we live, and he's gay so that's the reason for "Kewpie." His real name is John Small. He's six feet five inches and close to three hundred pounds so his whole life people have been calling him "Tiny" which he hates.

I'd been on the show almost four years before we said two words to each other. Basically, the train and the show are two different worlds. I mean you live on the train but, for the first couple of years on the show, it's pretty much a place to sleep and a way to get from closing at one site to opening at the next. Kewpie only sees a couple of performances a year. Taking care of the train, he says, is like running a prison—all the cells have to be clean, the place has to be secure, and all the inmates have to be settled where there's the least amount of friction between them, which is the biggest headache. Kewpie says that he's got no problem getting all the bodies onto the train, it's all the egos that won't fit.

My first couple of years on the show, I only would see him eating breakfast at the pie car. Every morning Kewpie would put away a couple of orders of steak and eggs, double hashbrowns, a stack of toast and, sometimes, hot cakes. I'd nibble at my dry toast and half-grapefruit, stealing glances at his table and he'd give me these glares whenever he caught me watching him. I thought he hated me for some reason.

Then close-and-move night in Chicago five years ago, about 2 A.M., I went back to the animal cars to see India before the train took off to Denver. The train crew had just finished loading. I slipped in to see India before they drew up all the loading ramps and closed the cars. I was a little drunk and I was standing next to her, talking to her—well, really crying against one of her forelegs and I heard this soft voice saying, "They're closing the cars, now."

I nearly jumped out of my skin.

Kewpie was standing at the back of the car, in the corner. "You're not supposed to be here in the first place."

"It's okay," I said, "they know me."

"I can see that." He walked toward me as he spoke. I think I should have been terrified—alone at 2 a.m. with this huge man who I thought hated me—but next to the elephants he looked shrunk down to normal size and his voice was almost shy-sounding. I said, "You don't belong here, either, do you?"

"No." Then I saw him smile for the first time ever and he said, "But they know me, too. We better go."

Then we walked back alongside the train while the crew threw the ramps up and locked down the cars.

"That big one. . . ."

"India," I said.

"India . . . do they all have names? I mean do they all know their names?"

"Of course. How else would they know who Karl's talking to?"

He shook his head. "I just didn't think they'd know. I mean I saw you crying and talking to that big one . . . India."

I felt my face getting red. I said, "Well, I'm a little drunk."

"I thought you were . . . either nuts or drunk," he looked down at me. "But I'm neither. And I saw her patting your back, like you were her kid. She knew what you were saying, didn't she?"

I looked up at him and I really started crying. Because it's a touchy subject with me. It's true, I talk to the elephants and they understand me. Okay, believe it or not. That's it. So you can see where I wouldn't want this to get around. I mean it's one thing to tell yourself an elephant is listening and understanding—you can kind of shake your head at yourself and say it's okay to pretend—but when someone else, someone you hardly know, tells you you're not crazy . . . well, with hearing that plus a little overdose of peppermint schnapps, I was standing there between the railroad sidings crying my eyes out.

Kewpie leaned down and hugged me and patted my back like India does. Then he must have realized what he was doing because he suddenly stopped patting and I felt this low vibration from his chest, like the kind of deep rumble the elephants make when they're happy to see you, and Kewpie tossed his head back and started laughing a big booming laugh. And then I was laughing too and then the train whistle let loose with its warning blast drowning out the both of us. The wheels lurched forward and we ran down to his car and hopped on.

We stayed up all night talking. Since most of the time the elephants are stabled backstage in the arenas, Kewpie only visited the elephants on the train. He said he liked to just stand in the corner of the car. Kewpie said he'd always been big, always felt like a freak. Standing there next to the elephants was the only time he felt normal. That was why he'd glare at me at breakfast, thinking I was staring at him like he was a pig. I told him how it was the opposite with me—I eat all day but I just can't force down more than a few bites at one sitting. Every meal I eat with other people they're always nagging at me to eat something. Suddenly we noticed it was morning and we were both starving. We headed down to the pie car for breakfast. Between his order and mine it looked like a normal breakfast for two and we've been eating together ever since.

It's Saturday night in Miami. That's three shows—one at 10 A.M., one at 2 P.M., and one at 7:30 P.M. We're all mashed into my room on the train, Donna, Kewpie, and me. Kewpie takes up a lot of room so that's why I say we're mashed into my room even though I have what they usually give out for doubles all to myself. As train purser, Kewpie makes the room assignments and ever since we became friends I had a double to myself.

It's almost midnight and we're sitting on my bunk across from the window, so we can see when the cab comes to get us. Kewpie is taking us out to the fizzies—that's the female impersonator show. Kewpie knows a lot of the "girls" in a lot of the fizzies. He doesn't date them but he'd like to. It's funny to see how shy a man that big can be. Kewpie and I go to the fizzies a lot. Donna'd never been.

We're watching MTV. A guy from the troupe that plays basketball on unicycles hooked up a satellite dish to the roof of one of the animal cars and charged five bucks a month for using it. First I told Donna we had cable. When she believed it I felt real bad. I usually don't think that kind of thing is funny but everyone seems to do it to Donna all the time.

Anyway, a Platinum Blonde video comes on, I think it was "Contact," and Kewpie says "Donna, that's you. Donna, you're on fucking television. That is you, isn't it?" and of course it is.

She looks better on TV even though they've got her dressed real trampy—black fishnet stockings, her hair teased up and plastered with mousse, way too much mascara, and some designer skintight whore-dog dress. I used to dress like that to make me look older when I was stripping. That's when I first started out. But being so short, it works backward on Donna so she looks maybe sixteen years old instead of twenty-six and I'm thinking to myself, now that's something to have—all those years back and not have to be so stupid through it all. Then Donna looks at the video and says "That's the guy who raped me." Not "That's the bastard. . . ." Not like it was tearing her up. Just like someone saying "Those are my shoes." I don't know who she was talking about. It wasn't one of the guys in the band, maybe a guy in the crew or one of the extras walking down the street. And like I'm sure I'm going to ask her "Which one?" I just sit there hoping that Kewpie doesn't either. Luckily the cab comes for us.

Donna doesn't go. She says how she figures that maybe the shows took more out of her than she thought. I feel like I ought to say something or stay with her but I really don't want to sit there alone with her.

The fizzies aren't any fun. Neither Kewpie or me can forget about Donna. Kewpie doesn't flirt with the boys like usual. He drinks a lot and gets all teary-eyed and starts muttering about what bastards men are. He sometimes gets that way and when he does I usually just get drunk and join in. But I don't feel like it tonight. We leave about a half-hour into the show and when we get back to the train Kewpie goes to pass out and I go down the corridor to Donna's room and knock real soft.

"Donna, you okay?" I whisper.

I hear the lock snap open and the door slide back. I see the peroxide blond hair.

"Donna's sleeping," Jared says. He looks me up and down. "Anything I can help you with?" He slides the door open halfway and stands there naked, grinning at me. Very funny.

I turn around and walk back to my room, listening to him laughing.

I don't have to bother asking about her and Jared. Donna is about to burst waiting for me to ask but a girl's affairs are her affairs, if you know what I mean, and I'm not one to stick my nose in.

Most of the time you stick your nose in, it gets chopped off. You get yourself involved with one of the other girls, start to feel like they're really your friend, and the next thing you know they're out dancing somewhere else or getting married to some lawyer from Vegas or going back to college, and you never hear from them again. I mean, how can they be your friend and never talk to you again?

Kewpie says the circus is like being on a merry-go-round. When you're in it, it's like you aren't even moving, you go around in your own little world and if you don't bother to look outside you don't get dizzy. Kewpie says the trick to being in the circus is to make believe you're standing in the middle of the merry-go-round and pretending the world is revolving around you. It's not like you never get to see outside people. Outsiders are always stopping in for a season or two— especially showgirls and clowns. And circus people leave for a while, too. But when it's time to get moving again, Lord help you if you try to hang on to something outside.

I didn't even date outsiders anymore. Like last year after opening night in New York, which is really a Big Deal, a guy comes backstage after the show and he is something. He has grey-black hair and a mustache and I swear he looks like Prince Rainier, only a lot taller. He's wearing a tuxedo and he has the biggest most gorgeous bouquet of roses and he says, "I'm looking for the tall red-haired dancer. Is she your sister?" My sister! I can feel myself stretching up as tall as five feet six inches can get. I tell him I'm the only redhead and how the costumes always make you look taller. He flashes his smile and I know he's practiced it a thousand times in front of a mirror but I *still* fall for it.

All that night I keep picturing exactly what his next move will be and saying to myself he's done this hundreds of times with a hundred different women but he is just so good—it's like watching Cyrus Frank on the Ball of Death, where he slips and everyone knows its just part of the act but you can't help gasping every time you see it.

We go out to a romantic French restaurant where he orders the most expensive dinner for both of us and he doesn't say a thing when I just pick at mine. Then he takes me dancing at a disco where we walk right through fifty people in line to get in. After that, we go to a private after-hours club filled with the most beautiful people, women *and* men, and everywhere we go somebody whisks away the roses telling me how beautiful they are. I keep feeling like a stand-in for somebody else who was *supposed* to be his date. I mean I'm no Grace Kelly.

Anyway, once the sun is streaming in over us at his hotel room and we're lying there on the giant bed and he already knows I'm really a redhead, all I do is ask him who the roses were really meant for and he about snaps my head off. And that was that. I got a lot of questions about when's Prince Charming coming around again which I didn't exactly appreciate.

So I don't stick my nose in about Donna and Jared. Of course I don't have to since Kathy let everyone know. Kathy's married to Karl, who I used to date. Plus she says she can't stand the sight or especially the smell of elephants. Me, I love it. That was one of the things I liked best about Karl—that vinegar smell of sweat and dusty hay and elephant leather. Now, he's got to shower with Lilacs and Roses for a half-hour before he can even go near Kathy. Plus she's a flat-out she-dog.

Kathy's been around. She's on her second hook-up with the show. Four years ago, when all the dancers in Vegas walked out on strike, she and a bunch of the girls left the show to work there. She's really built for Vegas—tall, thin, and blonde with great legs. She worked The Sands. I stopped by with Kewpie when we played there. Kathy gave us the grand tour and didn't I die when I saw the dressing rooms? I could still get in, Kathy told me. Since it was her that brought all the circus girls with her and saved their hides, they owed her a little something, she said, and just watch her pull some strings if I wanted her to. She knew I'd say no—the last thing I want in the world is to be obliged to Kathy for anything. I thought I'd probably regret it someday but I really never did. I'm a union girl and, dumb as it may sound now, I liked the circus. Besides, being head showgirl I had seniority and a little bit of pull myself which is why Kathy got on the show again.

When they settled the strike she was right back in Winter Quarters and you should have heard her whine how they dumped her and all the new girls she brought them. She's a good enough dancer so I didn't cut her in rehearsals.

With everything that happened with Karl, I should probably regret *that* part but I don't. Not really. If he was going to dump me for someone, I'm kind of glad it was for someone I *already* hated.

In Jacksonville I'm heading back to the train from the last show. We're off tomorrow and then we open in Greensboro. I hear Kathy calling me so I stop and she catches up with me. Her eyes are lit up and she's got her wicked little gossip smile. She can be a real bitch with that killer smile.

"Your friend Donna's doing the dyed blonde Elephant Man," Kathy tells me. This is the best little tidbit of dirt she's had in a couple of weeks.

"Tell me something new," I say and walk away across the arena. She doesn't say anything and all you can hear is my wood clogs go click-clack, click-clack real loud on the concrete. She doesn't try to follow me or anything, just waits in the centre of the arena until I get right by the exit. Then she says real loud, "I'll tell you something new. He's a great fuck."

"She's just saying that," is what Donna tells me. This is intermission second show Saturday in Greensboro. The two days here in Greensboro, it's been Jared, Jared, Jared, and I about have my fill of it by the end of the first show. So when she starts in at intermission, I tell her what Kathy said. She picks up my emery board and starts filing her nails. You know, the way the tough broads do in movies to show they couldn't care less.

"Anyway, I didn't realize you and Kathy were such good friends to go and talk about me behind my back."

Then right away I think, oh, Lord. I went and did it. Opened my big mouth and this is where it gets me.

"Why would she say it?" I say. Now why do I bother?

"She's jealous, that's why." Donna stops filing and looks at me real annoyed. "Jared doesn't even *like* Kathy. He would never go to bed with her. You should hear what he says about her. Says she thinks she's hot stuff but she wouldn't last two seconds in Vegas. Jared knows everyone in Vegas. Besides, do you honestly think I wouldn't know if Jared was sleeping around?"

First thing I want to do is tell her about my marriage. How you wouldn't know even if he's sleeping with someone who's supposed to be your best friend. How you can never know anything about anybody for sure. But I don't say anything. I'm sure it's written all over my face. I could use my emery board back about now.

Donna says, "Anyway, it doesn't matter to me if he *did*. We both slept around. Jared's got *plans* for us." And the way she says plans, this is a whole different girl talking. Like suddenly the tough movie broad is singing "Somewhere Over The Rainbow."

"Really?" I ask. And the question sort of hangs there.

Donna just laughs and tells me she wants me to see something.

We go to her room and she makes me wait outside. Then she opens the door and says, "Ta-daaaa."

She is wearing this spectacular blue satin show costume, with a matching headdress and fur-trimmed cape.

"Have you ever in your life seen anything so gorgeous?" Donna says. "Jared bought it for me in Greensboro from a woman who used to design for Broadway plays in New York." She looks like she's about to cry, she's so happy. She starts spinning around so the cape flares out behind her.

Okay, it was beautiful but first of all, she can't even wear it since all our costumes are production wardrobe and second of all, it's way too long in the torso, like it was made for one of those perfect Vegas girls. But Donna doesn't even care. She thinks Jared is God. What am I going to do, convince her?

I have had that done to me, my mother telling me Ray Blalock was a boy from bad seed and no crops come of bad seed. Ray Blalock, a boy who could moisten even Momma's eyes in church with "Amazing Grace," how come he couldn't touch her heart? I just didn't see how anybody who looked and talked and sang so much like Elvis could be so vile. Well, nobody knew about Elvis then. "Just wait, Momma," I told her. "Ray and me are going to New York. Wait 'til you see us both on Broadway. You'll see what happens."

"Don't wait," she'd said, "don't ever wait for a person to change. It's not going to happen."

"You'll see," I'd said. But it was me that saw.

"I got a job dancing," I told her on the phone. But I didn't say where. "Ray's been going to auditions all day every day and he's getting callbacks. Any day now. . . ."

And I waited for Ray's big break. I waited and my mother died and left me nothing but her last words on the phone, "I told you..." interrupted by the sound of my phone slamming down. Then it came down to rent money and Ray saying wasn't there any way I could make a little extra money at the club? And me coming home, clutching my first and only little bonus, finding him with one of the girls from the club—a girl I thought was my best friend.

To this day, I don't see how a boy who knew how a man should act could go ahead and do what's wrong. But at least I don't expect better any more.

So the next week I try and be extraspecial nice to Donna and I don't say a thing about Jared, even when he pats my rear in line for the pie car at lunch. I don't even turn around, just hiss at him that if he wants to keep his hands at all he better keep them to himself. He laughs his laugh and turns on that smile of his and I know he'd have done it again but then I see Kewpie and call him over to talk. Jared decides he's not so hungry any more.

Kewpie says, "Kathy tells me he beats up Donna."

I knew. I'm not stupid. Just because Kathy said it doesn't mean it has to be a lie.

By the time we hit New York, Donna and me are hardly talking. I'm sick of Jared and I'm sure she's sick of me being Chicken Little. Then everything changes.

Donna starts by telling me, "I guess you're curious where I've been keeping myself."

I say, "Not really."

She just ignores the cut. "Well, I started doing gymnastics again. The Oblockis are helping me."

"That's nice. Looks like they dropped you," Okay, I was being a bitch but it's true, she's got some nasty looking bruises. And not from gymnastics.

"Clumsy," is what she says. "I'm much better now."

I feel bad because here she's trying new stuff and her so-called boyfriend is beating her up. And here I am being mean. But I'm glad it's Donna. It's like she doesn't even hear it.

Donna says, "I want you to show me about the elephants."

I give her one dead look.

"Kewpie told me…" she says. Then she says, "Oh, shit. I know I'm not supposed to know. Don't tell him I told you. I promised I wouldn't. I swore."

"I'm going to kill him." I say that even though I know why Kewpie told her—it's been killing him seeing me lose a friend.

And Donna says, "Oh, please. Don't be mad at him. He was trying to help."

"Big help." I say.

"Look," she says, "You don't like Jared, I know, but this is crazy, sitting next to each other and looking away everytime one of us catches the other's eye, like we're strangers. I said something about it to Kewpie—he can't stand us fighting—and he just told me. They really understand you?"

I just shrug. "I think they do. I end up watching you all the time in menage, the way you are with India. God, I wish I could do that. Hey, I've got an idea. You show me about the elephants and I'll show you some gymnastics. I can teach you five or six tricks in no time."

"Teach an old lady like me tricks? I'd snap in half." And I'm thinking, "I'm the one can teach you about tricks."

Donna looks at me funny. "Old? That's what Jared said. He said if

I want to teach somebody I ought to try someone young like Kathy. I told him if that bitch wants to learn tricks she could join Carter's Dogs. Besides, what does she know about elephants?"

I laugh. "So you want us to do headstands on their trunks?"

Donna lights up. "That's a great idea!"

I almost choke.

"No, really," she says, "not on their trunks, on their backs. If the Bulgarians can do it on horses, it's a cinch we could do it on elephants. Do you think Karl would go for it?"

"You're crazy."

"Ask him. We can do it," she says. "Really."

Karl doesn't just agree, he's practically drooling. He grabs me and pulls me over to the elephants prop trunks. He starts digging inside, tossing out the sequined headdresses and harnesses, and pulls out a smaller, battered blue trunk. Inside he's got costumes and spears and ropes all rigged to look like vines. Karl's talking a mile-a-minute telling me about Tarzan-and-the-elephants vs. the Amazons. He's jumping around the floor, swinging from imaginary vines, fighting Amazons and elephants.

He's got to have had this act planned for years. I wonder if he was thinking of me when he came up with it. When he married Kathy he must have thought she'd be the feature. Of course one second after the wedding she let him know she didn't want anything to do with an elephant act. I bet he never even told her he had a feature act—just tucked it away for another season and kind of forgot about it.

We're in New York all May and most of June anyway, so we get permission to take the elephants outside under the West Side highway which is under repairs and we practice there.

This isn't as simple as it sounds. First of all, we've got to parade the elephants down 34th Street from Madison Square Gardens every morning around 6:00 A.M. when the traffic's not so bad. We had to get a police escort—two motorcycle cops—one ahead of us and one along the right side to keep people back.

The first time out, I showed up a little after 5:00 A.M. to help feed the herd—this was the first time in three years, since Karl and I broke up. Since he broke up with me. I didn't know how much I missed it. I mean feeding them. Not just because I like them so much, but I like to watch them put away the food. It's an incredible sight seeing them wrap their trunks around whole loaves of bread and toss it in their mouths like popcorn. They'll each put away a half-dozen loaves, fifty-sixty pounds of hay, a dozen onions, whole bunches of carrots, and bucket after bucket of water. When Karl and I were seeing each other he'd get mad at me for standing around not doing anything but watching—I wouldn't even realize I was doing it. I'd imagine how it was to be that big, picture myself with arms thick as elephant trunks, grabbing, squashing up whole loaves and popping them in my mouth. Me, who can't ever finish a meal.

It was kind of awkward that first day back. I'd ripped open one of the big plastic bakery bags and was tossing the loaves to the girls then stopping to watch them disappear and Karl started yelling at me as usual, out of habit I guess, before he realized it was three years later and we didn't talk that way to each other anymore. He stopped and looked at me, then just grunted and walked away. I watched him, laughing to myself but, when I went back to feeding the girls, I felt this lump in my throat.

The highway crews must not all have gotten the word we were coming or else maybe just seeing us was too much for them—twenty elephants, a couple of ya-hooing showgirls, and Karl with a couple of ringstock. A half-dozen guys in hardhats run out to the middle of the road and start pointing and shouting. A backhoe operator turns around to see what's the big deal and nearly runs them all down. Donna and I blow them kisses.

What's really great is to see the elephants once we get under the highway. All of a sudden there's this wide open space and big clumps of weeds which they rip out and chew up. The elephants all start playing around, getting really silly—I never saw them like that before—spinning around, trumpeting, picking up sticks and throwing them into the air. Even India, she's got to be close to sixty years old, she's swaying and flapping her ears and pretending to charge at the bridge supports.

Anyway, Donna did end up getting me to do some acrobatics, just a couple of simple tricks like handstands and walkovers, stuff I used to do back before I quit high school. But when I was doing them on India's back they looked really hard. At first, I was scared. It looked like a long way down off India's back and I didn't know how to fall without getting hurt. When I told her, Donna just looked at me like I was crazy. "You're not going to fall. Why would you think you're going to fall?"

Well, I fell. It wasn't the disaster and complete humiliation I thought it'd be. It's the part where Karl has "captured" and tamed India and I have to remount on Rama, the second biggest elephant. The way you mount is you say, "Down" and the elephant bends down, then you grab her ear, put your left foot on her knee and yell, "Lift!" then she raises her knee and throws her head back and you jump and straddle her neck. Well, what I didn't realize is Rama's actually stronger than India. So when she lifted and I did my usual jump, I went cartwheeling over the top. All these highway crew guys were watching us and when they saw me up in the air I heard this roar. I felt like I was in slow motion and I grabbed at Rama's back with my hands and tried to get my legs down onto her. Instead, I kind of half-twisted and slid straight down Rama's other side and landed right on my feet. Well, for a second or two. I actually hit so hard I bounced up and back down onto my butt. I just sat there on the ground kind of stunned. Then everybody started applauding and Donna was standing over me asking me where I learned that.

I thought teaching Donna was going to be easy. I mean, Donna liked elephants and, after all, what is there to teach? It took longer than I thought. Mostly, I think, the problem was my attitude. At first, I didn't feel right about the whole idea. Like it was something only I could do and I didn't want anybody else to know how. But then I'd watch Donna watching me when she was showing me the gymnastics. Whenever I got something right, her whole face would open up.

Another part of the problem was that I really didn't know what it was I did when I talked to elephants until I watched Donna try. Then I could tell her, too loud, or talk faster, or show her how to touch Sudesh's face when she was talking. Plus Sudesh just isn't as friendly as India—even with elephants.

"Look," Donna says, "maybe Sudesh just doesn't like me."

"Donna, if she didn't like you, I'd know. Look at her ears when you go up to her. See? They're relaxed."

"So she puts up with me. But you don't like me, do you, girl?" Donna says, stroking Sudesh's cheek. Sudesh just goes on eating. "I see India when you go up to her. She's reaching for you with her trunk and she makes that wierd purring noise."

"Give her time, Donna," I tell her. "You gotta start somewhere."

"How come there's no males?" Donna says, "I, you know, relate better with males." She waggles her eyebrows like Groucho Marx.

"I'll bet you do," I say like Groucho. "There's no males because that's the way elephants are in the wild—once the bulls grow up they go off by themselves and the females stay together like a family. They've got some males back in Winter Quarters but they can't keep them on the road. Karl told me India's son used to travel with them for years. Then one day he went into musth, which is like a yearly two-month sexual frenzy, and took off on a rampage into a town."

Donna gives me this astonished look. "Karl did that?"

I almost fall down laughing. I swear I can't tell if she is serious. Then I remember the rest of the story and stop laughing.

According to Karl, an elephant in musth is completely uncontrollable. India's son knocked over a car and ripped up a dozen trees and they finally had to shoot him. The show was forced to close and the town made them hire out a flatbed truck to haul the body away. When they brought the body back to the train, the driver parked the rig alongside the animal cars while the crew figured out where to put him. Then, this is what Karl told me, all the elephants came over and brushed their trunks over him and started tossing hay over the body like they were trying to bury it. He said he had a hell of a time pulling them away and

India refused to leave. She wouldn't let the ringstock anywhere near the body. Then she stood over the body and finished covering it up. Karl stayed up all night with her and in the morning she let him walk her back to the car.

I don't tell Donna, though. Maybe because it seems too much like the lies people are always telling her and laughing when she believes them.

Then, this was about the second week, Donna was talking to Sudesh and Sudesh snakes her trunk around Donna and strokes her behind the way they do. Donna feels this touch on her butt and jumps. I just start laughing and Donna's laughing and I feel really good for her.

This is the best time I have ever had on the show in the nine years I've been there. The elephants love it, too—getting the chance to be silly. I can see how Donna gets to know them and they trust her. Sudesh starts stretching out her trunk toward Donna as soon as she sees her coming.

Some TV news people hear about the rehearsals and they film us. That night we mash into my room again and watch us. We sit there laughing and drinking schnapps, yelling at the news, telling the reporters to shut the hell up. Then we're on and we all start screaming. They show the best part—the part where we're supposed to be Amazon queens having this war and there's Donna on Sudesh and me on India and we're charging right at Karl and Donna looks at me and I look at her with these murdering looks on our faces. I can see that light going on inside her like when she was dancing, getting carried away. Then I see me. I look at least five years younger. But that's not what surprises me. I can see it, that light, inside of me, too.

Jared ends up going out with us because, don't ask me why, Karl's gotten to be buddy-buddy with him. It's like Karl and Donna are the only ones who don't know what's going on behind their backs. Donna says Jared tells her I'm crazy—elephants are wild animals you're stupid to trust any wild animal that can kill you. And, okay, Jared doesn't hook them, not with Karl around but it's pretty obvious to me that he's been hooking them regular when Karl's not there. India gets in a panic when she goes by him, breathing hard, her eyes get real wide, her tail sticks straight out, and her ears are flattened back over my legs. I have to lean down and talk her back to normal. But all Karl sees is that they mind Jared real good and Karl starts giving him more and more stuff to do. By the end of the second week, Karl is having Jared do the Tarzan part two or three times a week.

So I ask Karl what's going on. Karl gets very excited, "The boss saw the TV news story and called me in. I thought I was going to catch heck but instead, we've got a show-spot guaranteed starting in Philadelphia."

"That's great, Karl." I give him a big hug.

Then he leans over close. "And the boss wasn't the only producer called me," he whispers. "I've had four calls from other producers. I'm going to use Jared to dupe this act." Meaning sell the same act to a bunch of different circuses. This is a very big deal because it can make your name everywhere. Like the Flying Wallendas with different Wallendas in lots of different shows or like when Emmett Kelly and his son were both doing the same clown act in different circuses.

I guess this must have been Jared's idea right from the start—getting Karl to dupe an act for him. So now I know Donna's big plans.

The next part is not my fault I don't care what Kathy said. This was the end of the last week of May, Karl comes up to me and says he's sorry but he's got to have me quit the act. I'm in shock. But Karl tells me Kathy, out of the blue, is jealous of me. Me. Like I did anything to make her jealous.

"Karl, what are you talking about? Didn't you tell her she's crazy?" I'm talking in this low quiet voice to keep from yelling at him.

Karl shrugs. "She's my wife."

That shuts me up. I press my lips so tight together they're almost numb.

But Karl just can't leave it alone. "To tell you the truth," he says, "I'm flattered." Then he turns his back on me and walks away.

I watch him for a second then everything explodes. "You bastard.

You let her think that, you big fucking coward." My voice gets louder and louder 'til I'm screaming at him. "You can't do this to me. This is my act." I'm standing there in the exit ramp of Madison Square Gardens listening to my voice ringing off the concrete. Karl doesn't even look back.

So I go to Kathy but she doesn't even want to talk about it.

"Kathy," I say. "You know I wouldn't do something like that."

"Maybe you would and maybe you wouldn't. That's not the point," she says.

"Well, what's the point?" I ask her.

"The point is people might *think* you are. And I am not going to let anyone say my husband is screwing somebody on the side and getting away with it."

"You've got to be kidding," I say. But I know she's not. "*What* people say I'm messing around with Karl?"

But she just says, "Oh, people. You know. Everybody."

And then, all of a sudden, guess who's taking my place in the act? Miss You've-Got-To-Be-Stupid-To-Want-To-Work-With-Elephants herself. Stupid, sure, unless you're going to be part of a featured act.

But what am I going to do about it? She's his wife. Oh, Donna was nice enough. She came up and told me she was sorry what happened to me. And I wasn't very nice to her even though I know she didn't have anything to do with it. Well, I was jealous. So I said something about *Jared* not complaining and that maybe it was his idea so's he could be with Kathy. And when the little dumbbell asked me what I meant, I pointed to her and went, "Dump de-dump dump Donna."

The next few weeks were bad for me. I had to see all the girls two or three times a day and I couldn't even look at them. Some of them were nice and tried to take my side but most of them weren't too crazy about me. Me, being the head showgirl and keeping to myself the way I do.

Donna just kept talking to me. Like you do with someone at a funeral to take their minds off it. And she meant to help but Donna's mouth is not exactly hooked up perfect with her brain. So pretty soon she'd mention what's going on with the act and then I'd snap at her to shut up. I'm not sorry about that. Everybody always told her to shut up and it wasn't like she took it hard. She just shut up.

Then one day she came in real late for the first show with the most godawful make-up you ever saw. Caked on. And it still just looked like a black eye with make-up. Well I don't have to ask who gave her that. I cleaned it all off and did what I could with it for her and it turned out good. You can get away with a lot in show make-up. But after the second show, I'm helping her put on her regular make-up and that is pretty much hopeless. And what doesn't help is Kathy coming by on her way out and saying, "Goodnight, Slugger."

Donna doesn't flinch. Donna is like a statue. But my hands are shaking mad. I could have killed Kathy right there and then. But you know what really makes me mad? Donna, just sitting there like it wasn't *her* boyfriend Kathy was screwing.

"How can you take that from her?" I yell at her.

"Take what? She was just joking," Donna says.

"Take anything," I say. "Don't you know what's going on with her and Jared? Everybody knows."

Donna just raises her eyebrows and points to her eye and smiles. That's what she does, she smiles.

Everything always seems to happen on moving nights. Especially after a long date in one place like New York. After a while, you get to feel a little bit at home there, even though you know it's not going to last. Like what Kewpie says about the merry-go-round—it starts up and you have to hop on and everything's a little dizzy at first. If you weren't born into the circus there's always a little reminder that you don't belong anywhere permanent any more. It used to be harder when I was a new girl and not used to always leaving.

What I did on close-and-move nights was I drank peppermint schnapps in my room and smoked too many cigarettes and listened to really sad music and cried. Not like real crying, just crying because it's what I always did. Like stretching exercises before the show.

So I'm probably listening to Joni Mitchell or Judy Collins when someone starts pounding on my door.

I jump right up. It's after midnight and I'm bawling away, trying to dry my face and I scream, "Go away!"

"Open up. It's John." That's Kewpie, what he calls himself when something's really important. Kewpie knows how much I hate for anyone to see me on moving nights so this has got to be important. I don't even say a word, just open up.

Kewpie is wild. He is crying way worse than me. "Come on," he says. "You've got to come with me." He grabs my wrist and pulls me out in the corridor.

"Just a second. I'm not even dressed." All I have on is a long nightshirt.

"Please." Kewpie begs me.

"Okay, okay. I have to get my shoes." I get them and I have to chase after him because he's already down the corridor heading toward the back exit. "What is it?"

"It's Donna. Come on."

Which is what I was afraid of. And then I hear the sirens. I go out after him, running hard and thinking horrible thoughts like Jared really did it to Donna this time or worse, she did something to herself. Right away I can see whatever it is happened down by the animal cars because there are lots of flashing lights. A few times I've seen a cop car with lights pull up. Maybe to break up fights with townies. A couple of times it was parties out of hand. Once, in Dallas, somebody gave them a tip and they arrested Tony King who was wanted for something or other. But never more than one car. Never an ambulance.

When we get there Kewpie crashes through the crowd of people. I slide in behind him but can't see anything except a big knot of cops and cop cars. Then I hear the elephants. I guess they must have been bellowing like that all along but I wasn't listening. I never heard them that loud before, one on top of the other. No one is even trying to calm them down. I hear India's scratchy trumpeting. It's frightening, almost a wild squeal. I run toward her and a cop starts shouting at me. When

I turn around, that's when I see Donna sitting half-inside one of the cop cars with the door open. She's looking down at her lap, holding Jared's elephant hook across her legs. Just looking, like the time with the black eye. India screams again, the cop is still yelling and coming after me, and I'm standing there, shaking, watching Donna. She's moving her mouth and I start walking that way to hear what she's saying but the cop grabs me.

Then I'm yelling, "Let go of me, asshole. That's my friend."

He's got a vise grip on my arm and a big hand on my back and he's talking to me like I'm a crazy woman, pulling me back into the crowd. Kewpie reaches out and plucks the cop's arms off me and says, "She's with me." The cop looks like he's going to get nasty but then there's a roar from the crowd. Everybody's staring at the open elephant car door, watching the people come out. Then, over all that, I hear somebody scream. It's Kathy. She's walking next to these two ambulance guys who come out of the car carrying a stretcher. There's a black body bag on it and there's blood all over the stretcher.

"Oh, Lord. It's Jared," I say.

Kewpie kind of whispers, "Not any more."

We stand there a long time. The ambulance leaves, the cops take Donna away and another couple of them ask us what we know but nobody says a thing. They leave and pretty soon everybody else does, too, except one cop at the door to the elephant car. They've quieted down some but I can still hear India squealing from time to time. I try to go in but he stops me.

"Please," I say, "just let me try to calm them down."

He looks around to make sure no one's watching and then slides open the door.

The first thing I see is the blood. It's everywhere.

"India."

I see her. She's spattered with blood, too. She looks crazy, white-eyed, at me. I call her again and again, louder. She's got her ears flapped forward like she's going to charge, swinging her trunk wildly and swaying back and forth. Then I'm getting pulled back, out of the car, the door slamming shut. I'm shouting her name into the cop's hand.

It took a couple of days until everything got sorted out and the show opened two days late in Philadelphia. I heard. I didn't go. I quit the show. Things were never going to be the same between me and India. And everything just felt wrong without Donna.

Donna was arrested and they were going to charge her with murder. But no one on the show would tell them anything and the cops ended up calling it an accident. Kewpie said the owners must have shelled out a lot of greasy green to keep it quiet. I don't know. I guess it's worth it to them not to have murderers on the show, even if it's just a showgirl. Not that she was on the show for one second after the cops let her out.

After everything happened, I went to the Manhattan Central jail to see her but when I got there, they'd already turned her loose. When I went back to the train, Kewpie said he hadn't seen her but her room had been cleaned out.

I finally tracked her down through the union. She's over at the Melody Burlesk. Stripping, if that's what you want to call it. Guys line up around the wall of this big room. There's a stage in the middle. You take off your clothes as fast as possible then they pass you around. You just go from one guy to the next when the lights flash in the room. They can put their hands about anywhere you let them—depends how much they tuck in your G-string.

I go down there to see her, and as soon as I step in the door I hear, "Nice tits, Red," and a pair of big hairy hands are groping me. I have to slug the guy who won't believe I don't work there. Donna is working the wall. She just looks blank, like someone scooped all the Donna out of her. I have to wait and watch her go through twenty-five, thirty guys before she gets her break.

I follow her backstage calling to her and she looks at me like she barely remembers me, like she hasn't seen me in years. She says, "Come on back here, I only get fifteen minutes," and goes into the bathroom. I start asking her how she is, where's she living, just talk. She has one leg up on the sink and she's washing herself where they grope her. I stop talking and kind of shudder. Donna says, "Oh, fine." Blah, blah, blah, while she's getting dressed. Then she stops, listening for the music.

"Donna," I say, "What happened?"

She doesn't say anything. Maybe I should have left it right there but I say, "Donna, I want to know."

Her voice goes real flat and quiet. "After the show, I'm back in Jared's room and someone starts beating on the door. I open it up and Karl is pointing his elephant gun in my face, screaming he's going to kill Jared. He says Kathy and Jared are going to Vegas to work Circus Circus and she's suing for half his elephants. He smacked her and she ran out so he came looking for Jared. Then he starts crying and he looks so pathetic I don't know what to do. I give him a drink and tell him I'll be right back. Then I go to warn Jared."

He was still loading elephants onto the train. She says, "I was laughing, telling him everything like it was one big joke and he just looks at me like I was some stranger. That's when he finally told me he was going to take Kathy with him in the dupe act. He just told me and went right on loading elephants."

When he put his hook down to tether them inside the train car is when Donna cracked. She slammed the sliding door shut and yanked the locking lever closed. Then she picked up the hook and started banging it on the side of the car, pounding and pounding the hook on the metal car walls, screaming and crying, scaring the elephants to death, with Jared locked up inside with them. Those tethers couldn't hold a scared horse not to mention an elephant. And there were four of them in there all going crazy with the noise.

Donna says, "My ears were hurting from the screaming—I wanted to make it stop. I had my hands on my ears. I was saying that. 'Stop.' That's how I knew it was me. Then I saw the hook in my hand. I stood there looking at the door. I was just looking at the door."

Donna stops and is looking down at her lap like the elephant hook's still there.

"Donna?" I say and she sort of comes to. She smiles at me like we do when we dance. A big frozen smile.

"Oh listen to me, jabbering about myself and I haven't found out a thing about you. What are you doing here? The show must be in California by now."

I tell her how I quit. How I've been working as a Rockette at Radio City. It's the same union. Rockettes, showgirls, and strippers. Lucky I had all that seniority because they have a waiting list a mile long for openings.

I say, "Hey, listen. I can talk to someone. See if I can get you bumped up on the list. And I've got this great place I sublet from one of the girls who's getting married. It's plenty big and it's rent-control and everything."

I look over at Donna but she isn't really listening.

I say, "Donna?" again.

She says, "I've got to go back on." She doesn't say anything else.

That's when I notice what she's wearing. That blue satin showgirl outfit Jared bought her. I start laughing but Donna looks at me like "What?" Like maybe there's a piece of toilet paper stuck to her shoe. She doesn't get it at all.

What I want to say to Donna right then is "I told you so" but the truth is I didn't. Knowing Donna, I don't think it would have made any difference. Once Jared got to her, with those plans of his, it was all over. Some people's dreams are more important to them than their lives. It's the same old story and I guess I should have seen it coming. Not that seeing it coming helps.

"Nothing," I say. "It's just good to see you."

"Yeah, me too. I gotta go, that's my music."

I start to go, back out through the big room. Creeps are yelling at me, "Down in front!" I just look over and give them the finger. Everyone is staring past me. Every guy in the place, guys with their hands all over the other girls, are all watching the stage. I turn around to take one last look. I didn't think I'd ever be back. Donna's up there, shaking and grinding, better than I ever did. Better than I ever saw. A real dancer in the middle of this slime-pit. But it's just the moves they're watching. It isn't the same Donna.

It's not as bad as I thought. Leaving the show, I mean. Donna was right about me not being too old—everything just got to be such a habit. The change is good for me. Sometimes I miss Kewpie real bad though. Sometimes I think about India, the way she looked at me, and I get the shivers.

There's always Donna. I see her almost every day but I don't even know why I bother. We talk and go out for lunch and I keep my mouth shut about making plans for the future. She still forgets her purse and loses her keys.

I walk her back to the Melody after lunch and she goes backstage. The creeps are still creeps but I stand there, in the back, ignoring them and wait for her to dance. I keep thinking I'll see it, where she forgets everything and the music gets inside her and something deep down clicks on.

Hell, I can wait. I'm not that old.

The Sliver

"Walter, stop picking. Will you stop picking already?"

That's my wife, Becky. I look down at my hand and there's the place where I've dug it away. I've been digging away at it again—the same place.

"I swear, Walter."

This is Becky again.

"You should go see a doctor about that. And I don't mean Dr. Felder, either."

Who's our family doctor.

She means a shrink because it's true, I sometimes dig into this hand now so bad that there are times when I have a hard time using it for a couple of days. It's mostly like a bad bruise from the pressure of my fingers clawing at it. Becky says I'm sure to infect it, but I say she's wrong. I'm very clean. I'm about the cleanest person I know.

This is what the shrink will tell me.

"You're not really looking for the sliver. You're not really digging up your hand, you're digging up your past, Walter."

Walter, not Mr. Wagstein.

Nobody calls me Mr. Wagstein.

Not even my bank.

This is funny—Becky is Mrs. Wagstein, but I'm Walter when the bank calls.

Yes, Doctor. I know, Doctor. Thank you, Doctor.

See, I was fixing the backyard fence. I hadn't touched it since a year after Becky and I were married.

Nine years.

The side boards looked fine—just grey with age and dried mud—but the top rails almost all needed replacing. The paint was peeling away and they were warped where the rain fell and stayed until the board edges dried and folded up.

Once that happens there's no stopping it.

I put in new top rails and sanded down the side boards, painting as I went. This is really the best way to go. Sand down a small section then paint it right up, piece by piece until you're done.

I'd finished the first section. It runs along the retaining wall six feet above the alley beside the house, along the walk where you enter from the front gate. It looked great. Really. I'd stop now and again, working on the back corner behind the lilac bushes, and just look at how nice it looked.

That's what I was doing, sanding, stopping, looking, sitting down behind the lilacs with my back against the fence, admiring my paint job, when the boards behind me gave way and I fell backwards through the fence and off the retaining wall. Right off the wall and six feet down into the alley.

It seemed so slow through the air.

I landed on my feet.

I stood there, tottering around, looking at the wall, and back at my feet. Then I started laughing. It was like a circus act.

Becky came out. She couldn't find me at first. I could hear her calling me.

"Walter? Walter? What's going on?"

But I couldn't stop laughing. Then she must have followed the sound because I saw her leaning over the top of the fence. I was trying to tell her the paint was wet but I couldn't squeeze the words out.

Becky kept talking, asking me what was going on, but she started laughing, too, watching me laugh. It was ridiculous. Neither of us could speak.

Then I rasped out, "Wet paint."

Becky looked down at her dress and saw the stripes of white against the dark blue silk and she stopped laughing.

Just stopped.

I stood there in the alley, tears running down, my whole face aching with the laughing.

"Stop it! Stop it, Walter."

Becky was screaming at me.

"Look at this. You've ruined my dress."

It was her best dress. She'd put on her best dress on a Sunday afternoon to go tell her lover she wasn't going to see him any more. And now it was striped with paint and I was staggering around the alley.

Laughing.

I could see how she must have felt and this brought me up short.

"Becky! Wait."

She was already in the house. She was standing in the bathroom in her bra and slip and heels, holding the dress out in front of her.

How do you take paint off silk?

She looked so beautiful.

I was thinking how I almost lost her.

Later, when Becky had gone out and I was back in the yard, down on my knees looking at the Walter-sized hole I'd fallen through, I discovered that all the side boards along the alley were rotten at the base. The boards were standing there fresh-painted, so smooth and straight along the top of the wall and right under the ground they were rotted away.

There wasn't much else I could do. I counted them up, measured them, went out to the lumber yard and bought new ones. Then I ripped up the whole length of fence boards and started replacing them, one by one.

I was working on the second section, where the hole had been and now there was nothing. I was hammering in the boards, and it was getting dark, and Becky wasn't home, and then the hammer slipped out of my hand and bounced off the wall and out into the alley.

I stood there looking at the hammer lying in the middle of the alley. Then I slammed my right hand down on top of the board and a huge, jagged sliver, two-and-a-half, three inches, sank into the heel of my hand.

God, it was horrible to look at—this sliver dangling out of my hand. I stared at it. I didn't feel a thing. There wasn't even a drop of blood. I remember thinking, "It's just a sliver, Walter."

I was looking at it like it was something else.

When I pulled it out it hurt like hell. The blood was pouring out and I went inside to clean it up. I ran into the bathroom and grabbed Becky's blue dress where she'd balled it up and thrown it away. I tore the sash off and tried to tie it around my wrist to stop the blood. Holding one end in my teeth and the other with my left hand.

I thought I was going to bleed to death. I really did.

By the time Becky got home it was dark. I was still outside sanding and painting, section by section.

I had a big wad of gauze on my hand and when I went to hold her— I didn't touch her, I reached out and around from about a foot back, I wanted to hold her so much, but I was full of paint and this was her second-best dress—that's when Becky noticed.

She took me inside and undressed me and then herself and we got in the shower together and she washed me clean and hard and she led me out and into bed, kissing my hand where the sliver had been.

There was a little trickle of blood that wouldn't stop but Becky didn't mind. She had my blood on her lips and on her breast where she pressed my hand.

Then we made love for a long time.

It was the best ever.

So please, no doctors.

I know.

I know I didn't get all that sliver. I was pulling out pieces of it for months.

I know when I'm digging there, what else it digs up, and when I notice the blood I stop.

It drives Becky crazy.

Skin Deep

Terry?"

The voice on the other end of the line was the dead man's.

"S'me. Joe."

Soft, babylike. It must be . . . four, five in the morning.

His voice was so undemanding, so familiar, I nearly forgot he was there. I was already drifting away, thinking who to tell that Joey was back. As if the news of his arrival had outgrown him. My god, it had only been a month since he'd skipped out on the circus and already his face was beginning to melt gently in memory. I tried to focus my thoughts on a face hopelessly overlaid with the brilliant colours and bold lines of the make-up that defined him better than his bare skin.

"Terry? Can you meet me at the lot? There's something I want to show you."

I dressed quickly, splashed a little water on my face and called a cab. When I stepped out of the motel into the predawn chill, every injury I'd ever had in my career responded with a stiffness and a dull ache. I shuffled across the street to the all-night truckstop where I sipped strong coffee and worried 'til the cab arrived.

I was sure he was dead. When he didn't turn up for the show in Chicago, I went to Mr. Fields myself.

"Some guys just get burned out," he told me. "Maybe it takes a week, sometimes a year, even a whole lifetime. I've seen it." He dismissed me with a wave of his hand.

I called the cops. Joey'd never missed a show in his life.

Everything about Joey was pure circus. His father was the star of the Flying Faronis, The Balancing Burnetts, The Fabulous Archer Brothers, and another half dozen troupes. Each act meant another bonus on the pay check. Joe Junior opened to a packed house on a Saturday night in Boston. He was born into it—not in a prop trunk, as the saying goes, but on one. Joe Giraldi, Senior, headliner of the George O. Fields Shows, delivered his only son between acts as his wife lay bleeding and screaming on that prop trunk.

I was there. When Joey was born, I'd been clowning for five years and had worked the Fields show ever since I broke into the circus. It was me who washed the blood away and put Joey to his mother's breast. By the end of the show, his mother, Luciana, was standing by the backstage curtain with Joey in her arms, pointing out his father in centre ring.

Nothing, not even the birth of his son, was as important to the Great Giraldi as the Act—a fact I'd learned the hard way in my first year as a clown. All First-of-Mays, on the road in their circus debuts, have high opinions of their talents, and I was no different. And no better. At that time, Joey's dad was performing a high dive into a tiny pool of water. I decided that the show needed a bit of comedy in the star act. After all, I'd been on the circus nearly six weeks and felt it was time I'd made my presence felt in centre ring.

For the show's finale, the Great Giraldi entered the ring, his sequined cape flashing in the spotlight. The spot followed him as he stripped to his diving trunks and ascended the narrow rope ladder to the high perch. I slipped into the cover of the darkened ring. A second spot lit the pool of water and the drum roll quickened as Giraldi stepped to the edge of the platform. He lifted up on his toes, raised his arms and the big top went silent. Just then, I popped up from inside the pool, spouting water from my mouth and scrubbing my bare back with a longhandled brush. The audience howled—a beautiful sound. Joe Senior howled; a deep, fierce animal sound that promised revenge. And later, after the act, backstage, I howled as the Great Giraldi lifted me up off the ground and cracked my ribs in his bare hands. But the broken ribs were merely the finish to the punishing look Giraldi gave me from the top of the perch.

A couple of months after Joey's birth, when Luciana was back in shape, the family left to form their own troupe. After all, Joe Senior was performing in over half the acts in the Fields show yet not one of the acts bore his name. With an army surplus parachute for a big top and a dozen hand-painted canvasses wrapped about poles, they could seat five hundred. There were twelve acts but only two performers putting on an incredible display of circus artistry and sheer endurance. They played all the little towns, papering their route with handbills and posters. When the weather held up, the crowds were usually big enough to fill the homemade tent. And whenever the Fields Show crossed its path, Circus Giraldi's attendance was swelled by another dozen of us on our off-nights.

It was on one of those nights, four years after they'd left the Fields Show, that Joey first performed professionally. He followed his father into the ring one night, unnoticed and innocent. As Joe Senior climbed the rope to the single trapeze, Joe Junior wandered beneath the swinging form, motioning his dad to wait for him. The crowd chuckled. His father began the act, kicking the trapeze into motion, and the laughter mounted as little Joey chased him from one end of the ring to the other. Puzzled and angered by the crowd's reaction, the trapeze artist put on a particularly brilliant and daring performance, transforming the laughs to gasps. But only momentarily. The laughter erupted again as the boy covered his eyes in fear for his father's safety. Joe Senior went right into the finale—swinging in ever widening arcs and suddenly leaping forward out from the trapeze bar. At the last second he caught himself by his heels. There was a satisfying scream of horror—followed the loudest laughs yet. As he swung upside down over the ring, Great Giraldi finally spotted his son beneath him, holding his shirt outstretched like a safety net. There was that look, the long silent gaze between them, quieting the audience for a moment. Joe Senior descended and grabbed his son. They bowed to deafening applause and Joey became a regular in the act.

From the audience it may have looked rehearsed, but up close the glare he gave his son was like that of a fanatical preacher whose sermon was interrupted by a drunken heretic. The fierce pride and maniacal drive that somehow kept the tiny Giraldi Circus on the road also twisted the lives of his son and wife. Perhaps it killed her. Joey felt it was his mother's death that changed his father. In fact, it merely removed the only obstacle to the old man's single-mindedness.

Luciana Giraldi seemed to all who worked with her a multifaceted gem. The tiny voluptuous body that radiated sexuality in her perform- ance was topped by an angelic face, glowing with sweet chastity and gentle humour. Yet, in practice with her husband, defending her son, she resembled a wolverine—her eyes flashing, attacking furiously as she stood her ground a full foot shorter than the Great Giraldi, arguing him to silence. Still, there was only so much she could do for Joey. Any son of Joe Giraldi was going to be a great performer. From the moment he could walk, his father began training him in circus skills, teaching him tricks of ever increasing difficulty until, by the time he was ten, Joey was able to perform nearly every trick his father could. Every mistake was met with that angry glare. Joey was not able to be a mere acrobat; he was to be a legend.

I was out of performing for at least two more months while I waited for a broken leg to heal. Luciana hired me as a tutor, despite the objections of Joe Senior. Ostensibly, I taught him academics. Luciana had managed to convince her husband that she was unqualified to meet government education regulations whereas I had a college degree. Secretly, Luciana's instructions to me were to show Joey how to be a clown.

The boredom of the previous month and a half was becoming unbearable and the delicious irony of transforming Joey into a foil for his father was irresistible. Besides, no other instructor would have lasted three days with the constant complaints and interference of the Great Giraldi.

Although I'd watched Joey grow up, I'd never spent more than a few minutes alone with him. At ten years old, he was oddly mature.

Physically, his strength and musculature were that of a teenager and with his relatively small frame the effect was an almost apelike appearance. Mentally and emotionally, he was a complete puzzle. Joey almost never spoke but his eyes followed every move with an intensity and a hint of amusement that was disconcerting. When he did speak, it was in a barrage of questions, observations and criticisms on a single subject, the object of his next act. If he played the foreman in the painter's gag, Joey needed to know what it was they were painting, how long the painters had worked together, who was the oldest—all points irrelevant to the performance itself. It was a kind of Method clowning and his assumption of various roles was remarkable for the nearly complete transformation of a young boy into a character. But it wasn't clowning.

Joey was adept enough. Yet there was an emptiness that somehow pervaded the swift skill of his moves. He was too good, all technical proficiency and no soul. As a student he was clever, skillful and astonishingly precise—a joy to work with. But he wasn't funny.

This was most apparent as he sat before a make-up mirror. Every day, he'd apply a new make-up like a painter searching for a subject, and every day he'd scrape it off and work the routines barefaced. Slowly, over the two months, his clowning began to develop into a character.

My leg healed and I went back with the George O. Fields Show, seeing Joey once or twice a month when our shows were nearby. His clowning was surreptitious, so subtle it was almost unnoticeable, and absolutely deadpan. Under his father's gaze, Joey's acrobatics were perfect, but once Joe Senior's head was turned—young Joey clowned. He worked without make-up or clown costume, of course, giving the impression that he was merely so absorbed in each trick that he failed to notice that he had tucked a climbing rope into his trunks or that his chalk-filled hands left handprints in embarrassing places.

Naturally, the laughter alerted Joe Senior that something was going on but Joey was so adept at covering up, it was months before his father realized what Joey was doing. He ranted, he threatened, he chased Joey across the fields of the Midwest promising murder but it was Luciana who prevailed, declaring she would retire if Joey were not allowed to continue. With only a cast of three, the Giraldi Circus relented and Joey was allowed to continue his antics—without make-up or costume.

Joey provided a perfect comedic counterpoint to the deadly seriousness of his father and the grace and sensuality of his mother. He learned to transform stumbles effortlessly into acrobatic miracles, cringing in mock fear of his father's anger at the blunder and beaming a smile of innocent delight and surprise upon landing on his feet. By the time he was thirteen, the rigid discipline of his father's training and the gentle encouragement of his mother put Joey well on his way to stardom. Stardom, not greatness.

I believe the adage that greatness arises from suffering. Despite the hardship of his father's tutelage, Joey was still a child, immortal, with life stretched out ahead of him in unending possibilities. His face, which he tried so hard and so unsuccessfully to paint, was unlined and still somewhat unformed. It refused to take the make-up as part of itself, giving the impression that the colours somehow floated on top of the skin like an oil slick on the ocean. Then, at the age of thirteen, Joey found his make-up.

The hard part of the act was over—he'd completed the two and a half flips from the trapeze to his father's hands, returned with one and a half twists to thundering applause. His parents had dropped to the net and completed their bows. Joey's descent was pure icing, the type of trick guaranteed to draw applause whether it succeeded or not. A double flip to the net, a bounce off the net and a slow flip back up to a sitting position in the catcher's trapeze.

Joey was still too small and light to make it all the way back up to the bar on his own. To provide the extra bounce, his father always stood beneath the net, holding it down. As Joey hit, he'd release the net, slingshotting Joey back up to the bar.

Joey isn't exactly sure what happened that night, he remembers finding himself flung off-course sideways away from the bar—and the safety net. His mother ran beneath him, arms outstretched, and he hit her, breaking her neck and killing her instantly.

The sun was nearly up when I got to the lot. The circus trucks showed flickers of light as the ringstock stirred awake for the morning animal feeding. A short distance from the trucks, the sleek lines of the performers' private trailers formed a darkened circle, but I knew Joey's wasn't among them. I surveyed the lot. It doglegged around a clump of trees to the east of the big top. Joey had to be holed up there.

He never parked with the others; he had to have a site rather than a parking spot. There had been times when I regretted giving up my trailer for motel rooms, but looking over these grounds I didn't miss it a bit. Old age has its comforts. Joey must have hated the lot. Nearly bare, the hardpacked dirt looked to be graded for a highway. Hundreds of little mud shows must have used it; bump-and-grind shows one week and a Bible-thumper the next, all leaving their own distinctive refuse behind. A rain would turn the field to mud broth, and fast-food wrappers would sink underground, layered over gospel tracts. On the open wound of the field the big top looked a brightly colored Band-Aid.

Raw earth, hedged by a line of dead poplars; round that, the field narrowed to a surprising slash of green. Poking over a rise in the grassy strip, I spotted the spires of Joey's trailer. In contrast to the streamlined contours of the Travel Queens and Winnebagos of the other performers, Joey had a museum piece—a mobile gingerbread house. He designed and built it himself, welded every joint of the undercarriage, carved the wooden frame and kept tinkering on it, changing it constantly. The wagon towered nearly twenty feet high and traveled down the road like a half-spun top, wobbling from side to side, always threatening to topple over. Cabinets, drawers, prop trunks, even a miniature merry-go-round were concealed in the truck's brightly painted panels.

Before the first show, locals would come out to the circus lot, gawking at the jugglers rehearsing between trailers, watching the ringstock shower and scrub the elephants, fascinated even by the exotic laundry that dried on the lines between trailers. Eventually someone would discover Joey's wagon parked away from the rest of the trailers and a crowd would ring the wagon, climb on it, run their hands over the curves of its elaborate volutes and wander around it reading stories into the clown figures carved in its borders. Only then, would the marvelous devices hidden within be revealed. Out in the lot, Joey's wagon worked a crowd the way Joey did in a ring—standing apart from the rest of the show, slowly gaining the attention of the audience and becoming its sole focus.

"Joey?"

I pounded the door and stepped back, looking for signs of life inside. Nothing. I walked around the wagon. There were no clues to where it had been the last month.

"Joey?"

"Damn, Terry. You want to wake everybody?"

I whirled around and yelled. A flesh vise clamped my mouth and another my arm. I stared into a gauze shroud.

One of the slits in the wrapping moved.

"S'Okay, Terry. S'me, Joe. An old fella like you shouldn't be getting so excited. C'mon inside. We can talk."

He turned, a living mummy, toward the wagon. I wondered what the hell had happened to him. Joey reached up, rapped the wagon hard and kicked something. Steps tumbled out of the undercarriage and the door popped open. The hand that guided me up the steps was strong and firm.

He flicked on the generator and the odd pattern of little spotlights illuminated portions of the trailer into its various "rooms."

"Joey, you all right? When you missed the show in Chicago we thought you were dead. We've had the cops out looking. . . ."

"I'm fine." His voice was steady, relaxed and soft. He gestured easily to the sofa. "Sit down. I'll make some coffee." He poured hot water over the grounds, dumped it all in the blender, whirled the contents a few seconds, then strained the coffee into two mugs. I missed all that: his strange approach to household chores, his little Rube Goldberg inventions, the odd logic of a clown in his home life.

I tried reading some kind of thought from the bandages that covered his face. Impossible. Only the eyes were all Joey, with an excitement not betrayed by his movements.

"Terry, I feel great. Better than ever. Here." I accepted the coffee. "I don't know, Terry, maybe it was being in Chicago. Remember when you used to work tent shows in Chicago instead of the damn concrete arenas?"

I realized I was straining to hear something Joey wasn't saying: I was leaning forward, half off the sofa, as though I could extract some extra information from his words. I scratched my neck and leaned back.

He cocked his head at an odd angle. I imagined the thin lips under the gauze stretching in a grin. "Remember the last time you saw me play Chicago."

The day his dad died in the ring.

It was the last leap of the teeterboard act. Joey had gone through all the antics, setting up the high perch on which he was to land. His father dropped onto the raised end of the board, vaulting Joey high into the air, entirely over the perch and landing him, as if by mistake, perfectly balanced on the tightwire. It was a heart attack, I suppose. By the time the applause stopped, Joe Giraldi Senior was dead. But it wasn't his final act.

Joey quickly slid down the guidewire and lifted the old man's body, bending it into a bow. I rushed down from the stands, looking around in disbelief at the crowd, still cheering in their ignorance of the death. Anywhere else, out of reach of Joey's casual covering movements, they could clearly have seen that here was a dead man draped over the shoulder of a clown.

I've seen circus deaths before. The call to clown alley has a hoarse tone of horror—"Clowns!"—and out we tumble to turn the collective terror of an audience into quiet reassured murmurs. It's all right. There was an accident but it will be fine. See, the show's still going on. The clowns wouldn't be out here if anyone was really dead. Would they?

But Joey's performance was something else. Nobody suspected the tragedy. And the show went on. Joey reappeared, setting up the next act—a ladder act. Dressed as a carpenter, he carried out the rotating ladder and toolbox, gesturing and shouting to someone behind him.

He stopped, set down his load and turned to yell at his partner, then realized there was no one behind him. With an angry gesture, Joey tramped back offstage and dragged out the body of his dead father, indicating to the crowd that his partner had been drinking.

I reached the backstage area and watched in horror as Joey manoeuvred the body so skillfully and comically that he seemed the straight man to the corpse. Constantly scolding and explaining, Joey set the body in numerous positions. Seated on the toolbox, it fell off. Leaning against the ladder it slowly sank into a heap. Joey motioned the dead man to go up the ladder. No response. He motioned again. Nothing. Lifting the body, Joey carried it up the ladder to midpoint, set the body in place and warned it not the move. He released his hold and watched the corpse slide down the rungs.

At last, again with the body draped over his shoulder, Joey climbed the rotating ladder and this time hooked the dead man's limbs around the rungs near the top. The weight of the two bodies at the ladder's far end set it in motion, son and dead father swinging toward the ground. Joey seemed unaware of the movement as he crawled "down" the ladder to its foot—which now pointed straight into the air. He reached the end, poking a cautious foot out, finding neither ground nor another rung. Joey swiveled his head about and, realizing his position, shrieked and leaped back to safety. His sudden actions set the ladder in motion. In mock terror, he began climbing frantically up and down the rungs, making the ladder rotate in ever accelerating circles. When the speed of the revolutions began to loosen the limbs of his father, Joey jumped off the ladder and stopped it with a jolt. The corpse was flung out through the air and right past me backstage. The last exit of Joe Giraldi Senior came amidst screaming laughter. The look Joey sent offstage, to the dead presence beside me, was the same look of anger that his father had given me the night I interrupted his act.

Yeah, I remembered Chicago. But I let it lie.

"Joey, what happened to your face?"

He rose and crossed to the dressing area of the trailer.

"I finished that show in Chicago. I finished the one when my Mom died, too. Never missed a performance before last month. But I couldn't go out there like this."

He touched the bandages, stroking the chin, the forehead, cautiously feeling the features of his face.

"You remember when my Mom died? Dad took us back out for our bows. Me in one arm in shock and Mom, dead, in the other. Thirteen years old. Why do you think he did that? Huh? For the applause? So the folks could see what they got for their money?" His soft voice rose to a shrill, cracked finish.

Joey swiveled back toward the wall, pulling a hidden drawer from the dressing table. The panelled wall above the dresser split open into a mirror. Joey rummaged in the drawer a second, digging out his sewing kit.

"Kind of makes you miss those old one-ring shows, don't it, Terry? But the good old days are gone. Now it's five-minutes-in-the-ring-and-out or the audience gets restless. Thank God for the three-ring circus. It gives the crowd a chance to change the channels, just like in their own homes."

I tried to imagine what could have put Joey's face in gauze. A fight? Not likely. Not all those bandages and it wasn't like Joey. Between his quick tongue and even quicker reflexes not many people could get to him. He wasn't volunteering any explanations.

"The bandages, Joey. You get hurt pretty bad?"

"Pretty bad."

He pulled the scissors from the sewing kit and peered into the mirror at his own mummy's head.

"You forget your ring's in a big top, not a boxing arena?"

"I guess I sort of wear my ring all the time."

He lifted the edge of the bandage from the end of his chin, yelping as the adhesive tore at the beard stubble below. Slipping the scissors into the gap, he began snipping the gauze.

"The new clowns you see today, Terry. This is just something to do for a year. Makes a great story to tell their buddies. Who in their right mind wants to be a clown these days, eh?"

Joey finished snipping through one side of the wrapping and started pulling the adhesive off the other side of his face. He stopped and swung around.

"You sorry, Terry? Ever think about all the things you never got to be?"

"Now and again."

"I never will." He turned back to the mirror. "You know what the final straw was? George O. Fields himself calls me into his office. I figure it's the usual, the Tzanotavis complaining about my ad-libbing with their horses, something like that. 'Sit down, my boy,' says the boss and I sink into one of those leather things in his office. 'Joey, your family and I go back a long way. Your daddy worked for my daddy and later for me. He was one of the greatest circus performers of our time.'

"I started to get itchy. I mean it was so damn funny and I gotta play it straight. 'Joey,' he says, 'I feel kind of like a father to you. I was there when you were born, I watched you grow up. Your daddy gave you the finest training he could. He wanted his son to be the best, just like he was. Two years ago, when your daddy died, I took you in and gave you a bigger role and more time in the ring than I've ever given any clown.'

"I almost laughed in his face but he kept rambling on. 'Now, I know you'd like a bigger spot in this show, but we both know that a circus is a business and it's the headline acts that sell tickets in this business.' He gave me one of those serious money looks he wears at contract time. 'Well, my boy, I've decided you're ready. I want you to headline for me just the way your daddy did.' Big Fat George grinned me a grin that would split a rock. I was outta breath. He gives me a meaty, sweaty handshake and pulls out a mock-up of a poster. 'How do you like this?' says he.

"I looked at the poster and saw my Dad staring back and, below the giant face, three rings of little Joe Giraldis doing all kinds of acrobatics, trapeze, ropewalking, you name it. I looked pretty hard.

" 'Scuse me, Mr. Fields, but . . .' I says and he laughs one of those oily chuckles and cuts me off.

"'I know,' he says, 'I neglected to mention salary. Why don't we just start by doubling the present amount?'

"'The money's fine,' I says, 'but the poster. . . . That's my Dad.' This really gets him and he about chokes to death laughing.

"'That's you, Joey,' he says and pushes the poster right up into my face.

"I stare at him and then stare at the poster and sure enough it does look more like me than my old man. 'But what about my make-up?' I says.

"'You aren't listening to me,' he says. 'You're going to be a headliner. Centre ring. No other acts going when you're on. . . .' I guess I was outta there and long gone by the time he finished."

Joey stopped and shook his head as if trying to make sense of that conversation. "I came backstage looking for you, Terry. Those other two clowns are back there. One of those bozos is standing at the phone booth in his skivvies. He's got his rubber nose lifted up on this forehead and he's screaming and cursing at his agent for not getting him some commercial as a dancing carrot. The other one's smoking a joint, talking to some showgirl about the psychological and sexual effects of wearing clown make-up and baggy pants. Jesus, Terry, I guess I was never smart enough to get that confused."

Joey cut through the last of the gauze.

I leaned forward off the sofa, craning to peer over his shoulder at the reflection in the mirror. The back of his head blocked my view. He pulled off the bandages. I heard the loud, clear peal of his laugh.

"You okay, Joey?"

He stood and turned toward me.

"I'm better, Terry. Much better."

Tattooed into his skin were the bright colours and contours of his make-up.

(for P.C.A.)

You Don't Know

We used to live in Chicago which I never much liked. Summers were always hot and humid and in winter the wind cut right through any protective clothing. Too many people, too much decay. Before we moved to Calgary, we were living in a small rented flat with most of our things in storage. Laura had insisted I sell the house. A Chicago police detective called us one day and told us they'd caught a burglar who had confessed to robbing our house. Why hadn't I reported a burglary? There must have been some mistake, I told him. Was my name Jeff? Was my wife's name Laura? Had I given her a silver and diamond necklace with an inscription on the clasp? The burglary had taken place more than a month before the phone call and we hadn't known. We weren't the first people not to know they'd been robbed, he explained. Especially when the guy was a real pro like the one they'd caught. But Laura made me sell the house. It made her feel violated and vulnerable she told me. What's the difference I asked. We'd been living there over a month since it happened and never even noticed. It was knowing, she said.

Things were never very pleasant in Chicago after that. Even for Laura. I got a great offer from The University of Calgary medical school and the Foothills Hospital Department of Pediatrics to be on staff and teach. Laura didn't want to leave but when she visited she liked Calgary. Walking around the neighbourhood of the hospital she saw a beautiful little house we eventually bought. It was bigger than the house in Chicago, but not too big. A nice family house that would be great for kids. She thought it was funny I was a pediatrician and didn't want kids. How can you tell other people how to take care of their kids. You don't know, she said. Not yet, I told her. I didn't feel we were ready.

I walked to work that day. I went home now along the winding sidewalks, feeling the warmth of the sunset on my back. I was surprised by the late September orange, red, and pale yellow-greens of the trees. When had they changed? I'd been planning to take Laura out to dinner, but I'd had to cancel when the clinic filled up at 5 o'clock. Laura said she'd microwave a slice of the frozen pizza we'd brought with us from Chicago. I said I'd grab a bite at the hospital cafeteria.

The streetlamp in front of the house was already on. Coming up the long stairs in the front yard I felt tired and had to rest. It was past 8 o'clock already, despite the sunset. I thought about when I could get to the yard work. The leaves were going to need raking and there was some kind of weed that had choked off and killed a bush in the hedge.

When I came inside, I could hear Joni Mitchell playing loudly, which is always a bad sign. Laura was in the TV room downstairs on the old armchair, with her legs drawn up under her, singing along and crying.

"Hi," I said.

Laura looked at me singing "and her heart is full and hollow like a cactus tree while she's so busy being free."

I hate it when she sings Joni Mitchell songs to me. I don't know what she's talking about. I sat on the padded armrest next to her and slid my hand over her shoulders. She hunched her shoulders and turned her head sideways and the muscles thumped against each other. Her shoulders hurt her all the time and she cracks them to relieve the ache. It just makes them worse in the long run.

"Like rocks," I said.

"Rocks," Laura said.

"So what happened?"

"Jerry hit Lucy over the head with a chair."

"What?"

"Lucy just called me from the hospital. They think she's got a concussion. They're going to admit her for observation."

"Is she alright?"

"No, she's not alright. Her husband hit her over the head with a goddamn chair and she's got a goddamn concussion. Does that sound alright to you?"

"Is anybody with her?"

"No. We live in Calgary, for God's sake."

"I mean does she have any friends who could be with her?"

"How should I know if she's got any friends? She doesn't have any family because her sister lives in goddamn Calgary."

"What hospital?"

"God. I didn't even ask."

"Probably Rush. She lives near there. I know some people at Rush. I'll call Bill Weddington," I said. "He'll look in on her."

"He's a pediatrician. You're a pediatrician. What do you know? You don't know."

I listened to the needle click click on the empty bands at the end of the Joni Mitchell record then I got up and turned it off. When I put the record away Laura said, "I don't want to hear any more Joni Mitchell."

"That's good."

Laura looked at me sharply.

"Can I get you anything?" I said.

"What?"

"You want some tea?"

"No, nothing. Do you think I should fly to Chicago?"

"No. I mean, did Lucy ask you to?"

"If Lucy asked me to, I would have been gone already. You would have got home and found a note," Laura said.

"Well, I'm going to have some tea."

"She shouldn't have to ask. I should just fly down."

"Don't."

"What do you mean don't?"

"I need some tea." I didn't want to have this conversation now. I knew what she was going to say and what I was going to say and how it'd end. I went upstairs to get my tea.

Laura was talking while the water ran into the electric kettle. Laura was talking when I plugged it in and the heating coils hissed and bubbled. She came up the stairs and the kettle began to whistle. I picked out something decaffeinated. I didn't want to be up all night.

"Jeff! Why don't you answer for God's sake?"

Laura stood at the top of the stairs glaring furiously at me. "You haven't heard a thing I've said."

"Honey, you know I can't hear anything with the racket that thing makes."

"You weren't listening."

"I was listening but you were downstairs and the kettle was on." I squeezed the tea bag and tossed it into the garbage. "What were you saying?"

"You don't care."

"If I didn't care I wouldn't ask."

"It doesn't mean anything when you ask. You just ask because you think you should ask. You asked me if I would mind moving to Calgary, and I told you I would damn well mind and did you care?" Laura said.

"No."

"What did she do?"

"What are you talking about?"

"I was wondering about your sister."

"What do you mean what did she do?"

"I can't imagine Jerry hitting Lucy with a chair."

"Well, he did."

"But can you imagine? Jerry?"

Laura looked at me with her head twisted. I thought she was going to crack her shoulders again but she was just looking. Like she was a bird and I was a worm.

"You think he had a reason."

"He had to have a reason. I mean, Jerry, after all."

"You're as sick a bastard as he is. You really think there is a reason, any reason, to hit someone over the head with a chair?" Laura was shaking mad.

"Let's sit down, honey." I tried to slip my arm around her waist and move her into the living room but she hit my arm. Hard. Tea splashed onto the saucer. I went ahead and sat down in my chair. I blew on the tea and listened to Laura rattle bottles on the refrigerator door. Something would fall when she slammed it. Oyster sauce. She would clean it up right away and somehow that would calm her down.

"Honey," I said. "Remember the oyster sauce."

"I'm not going to slam the door. Okay? Some of us learn from our mistakes."

Laura brought me some cut up lemon. I wanted to hug her but she'd just push my arm away. She was thinking of something else. Standing by the chair, holding the plate with the lemon, looking out the picture window. Weak orange sunlight seeped in now the trees were half-bare. Tiny threads and dust motes hung in the light beams. I looked at them and wondered what kept them up. Just waiting out Laura. The plate in her hand dipped and I finally reached up and took it from her.

"Thanks, honey. I love you," I told her.

Now she started to cry. I put the cup and the plate of lemons down, stood and hugged her, running my hand over her aching neck and letting her rich brown hair slip smooth and cool through my fingers. She dug her face into my chest, wrapped her arms around my bony hips and hugged me back, smelling like cashews and lemons, crying in the light shafts.

"How can you think there's a reason?" Laura said. "It's not like you."

"To think he must have a reason? I'm not saying he's got any excuse for hitting her. But what can possibly have gone through his mind?"

"I've never trusted him."

"Jerry? He does all our taxes, he wrote our wills, he makes most of our investments."

"It's not the same," Laura said. "When it comes to love it isn't the same. Some men act crazy when it comes to love. You're not like that. You don't know. You would never hit me over the head with a chair."

"No."

"Just yourself."

I didn't say anything. I knew what she was talking about but I didn't say anything.

Laura started laughing. I loved to hear her laugh. It was a low, sexy, throaty laugh. In college, when she asked me why I loved, her I used to say it was because of her laugh and the way she smelled like roasted cashews. "You remember when you hit yourself with the chair?" Laura asked.

"Yes." I held her close and inhaled. "Let's go to bed."

Laura pulled back and looked at me. We hadn't made love in a month. My fault. Too much work, I'd told her. Too much work, too many distractions. Too many unhappy stories from unhappy parents of every patient I'd examined.

In bed, Laura said she couldn't. She was thinking about Lucy and Jerry.

"I think she should call Sol Epstein," Laura said. "Jeff? Don't you think she should call Sol Epstein? What are you thinking about?"

"Why should she call Sol?"

"Because he's a friend and a killer divorce lawyer."

"What makes you think she wants to divorce Jerry?"

"Come on."

"Come on?"

"She'd have to be crazy to go back with him. My sister is not crazy. A little impulsive, a little wild, but not crazy. She is not one of those women who could just forgive and forget."

"How could that happen?" I said. "They've been together four years."

"Five. Married four."

"Five years and suddenly he hits her with a chair?"

"He was trying to kill her."

"You really think they'll get divorced?" I asked.

"Some things you just can't patch up. Some things just are so bad you can't fix them. How could she ever feel safe again? She'd never know if he was going to go after her. She wants kids, for God's sake. You think it would be a good idea for her to have kids with a man who tried to crush her skull?"

"And you don't think she did anything to provoke him?"

"What could possibly provoke any sane person to hit somebody over the head with a chair?"

"Bob Marcus," I whispered.

"What?!" Laura sat up in the water bed.

"I just wondered if maybe she'd had an affair,"

"You said Robert Marcus."

"I was thinking about Lucy."

"No you weren't. You were thinking about me. You were talking about Robert and me like you thought I was having an affair. Like something that happened fifteen years ago. . . ."

"I was thinking that if Jerry was as jealous of Lucy as I am of you, he might be crazy enough to hit her."

"We weren't even married," Laura said.

"We were living together."

"It lasted a total of one week," Laura said.

"Because he left school."

"He left school because I told him I loved you and not him, and I wasn't going to see him ever again. My God, I never should have ever told you. You never would have known. How can you possibly be throwing this in my face now?"

"I'm not throwing it in your face."

"The hell you aren't."

"You asked why would anybody hit someone with a chair."

"You didn't hit me with a chair."

"No," I said. "I hit myself."

"What are you talking about? You didn't hit yourself with a chair because of Robert. That was months after Robert. It was months after I even told you about Robert. You hit yourself because I beat you on a biology test, don't you remember? We both took biology together and I beat you on the final. Then we swore we'd never take another course together. We were too competitive. Don't you remember anything?"

I remembered how it felt. I picked up the huge rocking chair we'd refinished and mistakenly revarnished orange. I held it above my head and Laura must have thought I was going to throw it at her because she screamed and ran. Then I just opened my fingers. The chair dropped onto my head, hit, and slid forward onto the apartment floor. I remember the thunk. The sound of it going right through me. Then I wasn't thinking. There was this one thunk of not thinking about anything. An incredible sound. There wasn't any blood. Everything returned to normal seconds later and we swore we'd never take another course together. But I'd been thinking about Bob Marcus.

Laura said, "Jeff? I thought I was in love with him, you know. I thought I really was. I didn't even know myself how much I loved you. I never would have known unless it happened. I would have always wondered. I really do love you. You know that, don't you. That couldn't ever happen now." She curled sideways, sliding her leg across my legs. She nuzzled her face into the hair on my chest and ran her hand lightly along my side. She likes to listen to my heart beat.

I lay on my back looking at the ceiling. I ran my hands over Laura, savoring the feel of her skin, the curves of her back. Gently, I began to massage the knots in her shoulder. I do this every night. They were harder than usual. Usually they respond to a strong, steady pressure, the knots melting away under my fingers. But they didn't. She was still thinking about Lucy.

"Stop," she whispered.

I relaxed my fingers and just held her. We lay like that for a long time. Then I felt the muscles thump as she hunched her shoulders to relieve the ache.

When her breathing grew long and regular, I brushed Laura's hair around the shell of her ear and whispered, "I believe you. Even if you don't." Laura mumbled something in her sleep and rolled over, clutching her pillow between her breasts.

I slid out of bed and put on a bathrobe and slippers. I went down the hall into the living room. The big window behind me rattled with a sudden gust of wind. I turned, looking down the slope of the yard. It must have been one single blast of wind. Elm leaves were showering around the trunk. I thought about kids playing in the leaves.

I went to the door and opened it. It seemed warmer outside. I went out and walked across the crest of the lawn to where it sloped off suddenly. Then I turned and looked back at the house.

The weed in the hedge was only three feet high with no more than seven or eight waxy leaves clinging to three twisted stalks. I went over to it, grabbed two of the branches and pulled. It lifted slightly and when I pulled again, I could feel the earth giving way under my slippers before the limbs snapped off. The one remaining stalk bent, twisted, yielded its single leaf but didn't come out.

I went into the garage, got out the spade, and started to dig at the weed's single root. It was like a jungle vine, sinewy, and incredibly strong. I dug until I came to where it tangled with the mesh-like roots of the hedge bushes. Some of them were already torn by the spade.

I knelt and found a narrow spot where I gripped the root and bent it, trying to snap it in half. It cracked, giving off the acrid scent of green olives but refused to break. I crimped the root double, twisted and folded it over and over. The damn thing wouldn't break.

I didn't hear the car pull up, didn't hear the doors open. The whole front of the house exploded in light. My shadow zigzagged across the slats of aluminum siding, hacking down again and again with the spade like the shower scene out of *Psycho*. I turned, blinded by the floodlight from the police car, my bathrobe thrown open, screaming down at the cops, "We're going to live in this house!"

Laughing Sickness

People don't understand about us, how we walk out of one world and into the next. It takes practice and some people just never can do it. You can teach people clown gags all you want but it doesn't mean they're going to learn anything about being a clown. I never did. I'd say everything I know I learned from Mary.

First time I saw her was during a high wire act at The Great New Yankeeland Circus in a little town a hundred twenty-five miles east of Boston. She was dressed like an undertaker and driving a tiny hearse, waiting for the wirewalker to die. It was the funniest damn thing I'd ever seen.

We'd just closed Boston and I was on a three day break with all the other clowns from the Big Show before we opened New York. So, naturally, we piled into Jonesy's VW van and drove a hundred twenty-five miles to see another circus. The other clowns, the Oldtimers, had worked with Mary in some show or other over the years—she'd worked twenty shows in as many years. All I'd heard about her were the stories they told at the Saturday bull-sessions in the back of the Oldtimer's train car, the Too Loose Caboose.

I didn't really belong there. I was a new clown, a kind of experiment. The Big Show had always fielded at least ten clowns, veterans from the little shows who'd worked their way up, but after the last tour, one had retired, one had died, and another was up on morals charges in Florida. Rather than hiring a bunch of aging clowns from other circuses, they decided to start recruiting and training their own clowns. Me.

During those first few months with the Big Show, I'd kind of attached myself to Billy, a sixty-year-old fat dwarf. I'm six feet two inches and 190 pounds, so I looked monstrous next to him. Funny thing was, wherever we went, I was always running to keep up with him. Billy was incredibly fast with his beachball body and his stumpy little legs. We'd weave our way through crowds and Billy'd talk about how he'd worked this tent show or that, mud shows he called them, when he first broke in. His large, lumpy head would tilt forward as he walked, his mouth always going, as if the speed of his feet and his mouth could distract attention from his appearance. I'd smile and say nothing. I liked the stares. Just being beside the old dwarf made me a kind of mystery, half-in, half-out of the circus.

That Saturday night I'd followed Billy into the Too Loose Caboose. He was saying, "I ever tell you guys the time Mary worked the Forepaugh-Sells show with me? She's a handsome woman, so they was always trying to make her fill in as showgirl. She's supposed to ride lead elephant in opening, wearing one of those ass-crack sequin jobs, waving and smiling. Can you imagine? Mary. I mean you could hear that girl backstage swearing fit to make a trooper blush. But hell, you ever read your contract? It don't say you're a clown. Just a employee. So opening night she rides in without the costume doing Lady Godiva. She's got on this six-foot blonde wig and nothing else. I tell you. The ringmaster himself don't know what's going on. He's still doing his spiel and in that show, I swear, it goes 'Ladies and Gents. Forepaugh-Sells Combined Shows reveal to you the wonders of the circus world.' Hundreds of wives are beating on their old man trying to get him to take her and the kids home. And I hear when they finally found her she was still on top of the elephant, only she's got this flyer with her. . . . " And then everyone started screaming at him.

That was part of the routine. Whenever the Mary stories started in on her sexual exploits, which they always did, everybody would shout down the storyteller, leaving Mary locked naked in the Clown Car in centre ring or hiding from a Bulgarian weight-lifting bisexual under his lover's bunk. The Oldtimers all knew those stories but all I'd heard were the preliminaries, titillating scenarios of Mary in various stages of undress, experimenting with alternative uses for rubber noses or foam props, that ended with lewd winks and leers from the storyteller.

Jonesy said he was starting the three day holiday by taking his old VW microbus for a drive to the Great New Yankeeland Circus, Mary's new gig, and he offered rides to the rest of the Oldtimers. The others were all for it only Jonesy didn't even look at me. It was Billy who convinced them to let me in.

So the next morning a dozen of us headed for New Yankeeland. It was crowded, but not too bad, until we got off the highways and onto a little dirt road which was seriously pitted from a week's heavy rains. Jonesy's shocks were about gone and I was at the bottom of the pile feeling every bump on the road and every squirm from the clowns above me. I had to scrape myself off the floor when we stopped.

There were three tents—a menagerie, the sideshow, and a beautiful old Big Top. When I'd joined the Big Show it had already moved from tents to the indoor arenas, and I was like a little kid looking at this set-up. The red-white-and-blue-striped tents stood in a grassy meadow with a thick pine forest behind them. There were American flags and red-white-and-blue banners flapping in the breeze. It looked liked something out of a hundred-year-old painting. We wandered with the Sunday matinee crowd under a painted archway that read "The Great New Yankeeland Circus."

We went into the Big Top and the Oldtimers wrangled us front row freebies. I realized it had been a long time since I'd seen a circus from the outside and, even though I'd been doing thirteen shows a week for twenty weeks, I was just staring at everything like I'd never seen it before.

They opened big—with a solo high-wire act. The wirewalker climbed to the high perch and then a miniature black hearse raced into the ring raising a cloud of sawdust, belching black smoke and backfiring. It stopped in centre ring, a door opened and out popped a wide black clown shoe at the end of a black-clothed leg that stretched nearly as long as the car. Billy dug an elbow in my ribs and hissed "That's her."

Mary squeezed out of the car and stood up, dressed in a black tuxedo. In the oversized undertaker's top hat, she must have been nearly seven feet tall. She had a simple character make-up—just a couple of black smudges for eyebrows set low on her forehead, a reddened W.C. Fields-type putty nose, some white highlights around the eyes, and a lower lip done in black rather than red. The corners of her lip drooped down so that when her mouth was relaxed she had a permanent scowl and when she smiled, she smirked. A wiseguy. The wirewalker eased onto the tightwire. Mary eyed him professionally. She brought out a pad of paper and scribbled something, stopping from time to time as if she was devising some complicated scheme. Then she snapped the pad shut, knelt down, and drew a long coffin shape in the sawdust. She got up and leaned against her car, waiting for the wirewalker to fall into the area she'd marked. He completely ignored her and went through his routine, finishing with the most dangerous tricks and taking his applause. Meanwhile, Mary was checking an imaginary watch, tapping her foot, motioning to the audience that it'd be any second now. The wirewalker had already finished his act and was sliding down the guy wire. When she finally got fed up waiting, Mary looked up at the empty wire overhead. She gave a nod like this was what she'd expected and looked down into the coffin she'd drawn.

She did a great take of complete shock and surprise then went down on all fours, searching the sawdust for a corpse. The wirewalker stepped behind her and peeked over her shoulder. Mary backed into him and turned around to explain what she was doing. There was a slow moment of realization and then a perfect doubletake as she recognized him. She looked down at the empty coffin, back to the wirewalker, and started berating him, ordering him to fall down dead in the coffin. He laughed and walked away with Mary shaking her fist at him. Then she climbed back in the hearse, slammed the door shut, and drove off.

All through the show, Mary returned during the most dangerous acts, sizing up the performers but never managing to land a corpse. During the tiger act, she measured the trainer and drew his burial plot but, after seeing him wrestle one of his tigers to the ground, she erased it and laid out plots for each of the tigers. As each act finished, Mary got madder and madder, chasing after the performers and kicking at the sawdust coffins.

The show's finale was a human cannonball act performed very simply. The ringmaster announced the Great Zefferelli and a single spot hit Ring One. Zefferelli, his lovely assistant, and an enormous black cannon were the only things lit in the Big Top. He crossed himself, climbed inside the huge cannon muzzle and his assistant lit the rear fuse. A second spot suddenly flashed to the far end of the Big Top as a deafening explosion and burst of fire and smoke shot out the rear of the cannon. The human cannonball stretched out in a swan dive. He flew down toward the safety net, curling his body to cushion the shock, but a huge black shape blocked his path. Mary, holding up a balsa wood coffin suspended from two long poles. Zefferelli smashed through the box safely into the net and bounced to his feet. The crowd gave him a standing ovation.

Mary gave the crowd a disgusted look and turned to leave but found herself surrounded by the whole cast. There was an inner ring of performers whose acts she had interrupted. They carried a coffin. Mary grinned weakly at the mob. They set down the coffin. Mary gestured, "For me?" The cast all nodded. She shrugged, stepped into the box, and brought a large, real-looking handgun to her temple. She pulled the trigger. There were nervous laughs from the audience as the gun went off and she sank into the box. The mob closed in and six performers bent and lifted the coffin high into the air. Together, the cast began a slow funeral march. As they moved forward, you could see they'd lifted a bottomless coffin. Mary lay in the centre of the ring, hands still folded neatly across her chest. When the last of the performers had left the ring, Mary sat upright and waved wildly at them as they crossed the track surrounding the rings and continued toward the exit. Then, with a short shrug, she ran after her own funeral. All that was left were the three empty rings. The spotlights went out and the house lights came on.

The strangest part for me was that the entire audience understood that the circus was over. The ringmaster didn't come on and thank everyone for coming. There was no musical theme, they didn't have the final parade by the stars in their sequined costumes; just the slow funeral march, chased by its guest of honour.

The other clowns and I looked at one another. They must've seen dozens of circuses together over the years; any nearby show on a day off was like a family reunion for them. Which didn't mean they'd have anything good to say about the shows they visited. The moment a show ended, they would tear into the clown acts, shredding the performances for even a single mistake. But this performance left us all speechless. We went backstage as open-jawed as any eight year-old kid.

Backstage, I felt completely alone. I didn't know a soul from the New Yankeeland crowd and the clowns from the Big Show treated me like a bastard at the family reunion. I watched Mary. She shook a few hands, kissed a few cheeks then slipped out. I followed her out the rear of the Big Top toward the trailers. I don't remember what I said. If I'd thought about it I'd probably never have said anything but I was still feeling half-dazed from the performance and the backstage party. She turned and looked at me. Mary was tall—about six feet—thin but not skinny. Strong. She gave me a long look up and down then tossed her head for me to follow.

Her trailer was a surprise. Clown rooms on the train were covered with all kinds of circus stuff, posters, snapshots, route cards, but Mary's was beautiful, sparkling clean, and decorated like a model apartment. The little furniture she had—a make-up table, two rugs, a coffee table, sofa and matching armchair, a kitchen table with two matching chairs— was arranged to break up the rectangular space into little "rooms."

"Take a seat," she said. I sat on the sofa, feeling like my sweating palms might stain the upholstery. I fumbled with my hands and finally folded them in my lap.

Mary excused herself and stepped into the bathroom. Across from the sofa was a huge mirror, seven by seven at least. I tried to look casual, leaning back, resting one arm on the sofa's end, crossing then uncrossing my legs. There were just two framed pictures on the walls. One was a print of some famous artist's self-portrait. The other was a black-and-white photo of a young woman's face, in the same pose as artist's, with the same expression of despair.

Mary came out wearing a purple terrycloth robe. She hung the tuxedo neatly in the closet and sat herself in front of the make-up table and mirror at the far end of the trailer, not saying anything. I'd seen that look before. You finish a show and walk backstage and it's like you're barely in touch with the world. Everything seems dead, sitting in front of the mirror, looking at the make-up, all smeared and cracked. Just for one second the thought crosses your mind: "What if I didn't take it off?" Mary sat and stared in the mirror, then stripped off her wig. She tucked a couple of stray hairs back into the hair net, dipped her hands into a jar of coldcream, and began rubbing the stuff into her face, turning the sharp make-up lines into a slimy maroon mask.

"This is really a nice place. I'd never have guessed, just looking at it, you were in the circus."

She looked at me oddly. "Thanks, I think. What's on your mind?"

"I'm on the Big Show. . . . "

"I know. What do you want?"

"Nothing. I guess I just wanted to meet you. You know I've heard all these stories. . . .

"Hmmm." She continued stripping the make-up off, burying her face in a wet cloth.

I was really squirming, babbling almost. "That show was great. I just wish I could do something like that."

Mary finished scrubbing off the grease. Her skin looked soft, very pale, tightly drawn. What was she, forty? Fifty? She didn't look it. "Why don't you?" she asked.

"Well, first of all, they don't let new guys ad-lib on the Big Show and, second of all, they don't let anybody ad-lib on the Big Show."

Mary laughed. At last. "So what have you got to lose?"

"What do you mean?"

"Just what are you going to lose by improvising?"

"My job for starters."

She shrugged and turned back to the mirror. She pulled off her hair net and a mass of black and gray curls shot out in all directions, like a mushroom cloud around her head, settling under their own weight to her shoulders.

"What do you want me to do? Quit?" I asked.

She swung around. "I don't want you to do anything. You're the one who said he'd like to do what I do. The way I see things, you can only really lose what you've earned and from what you're telling me you haven't earned a damn thing yet. You get your ass kicked out of the Big Show and work your way back into it. Then you've got something to lose. You think you're gonna learn something from the clowns you work with? You're lucky if those bastards don't cut off your nuts."

"I keep my eyes open."

"Well, that qualifies you to be a professional audience member, at least. And God knows we need them," Mary laughed. "You learn anything watching me?"

"I don't know. I couldn't get away with doing what you do. Working off the acts? I already took some heat for trying that."

Mary spun around on the chair and leaned over eagerly. "Really? Tell me."

"See, for the clown spot, I do this comedy juggling gag. I follow the big cat act. The tamer always takes about twenty bows on his way out so by the time I can get my bit started, half my time is gone. So I brought out a stuffed lion one day, threw it into the juggling act and ended up wrestling with it on the ground. The rest of the time I spent taking bows."

Mary was listening with a half-smile on her face. "And then. . . ?"

"Not much, I guess." I was squirming again. "I never really got a chance to work it. It got some good laughs but the tamer complained. He had friends in management. You know. Next thing I know, the performance director is telling me to knock it off."

"What were you doing?"

"Just trying to make him stay out of my time slot. Hey, it worked. He must have knocked off ten bows."

Mary sat back on the chair. "Jesus, if that's all you wanted, why didn't you just ask him to cut it short in the first place?"

"Like he's going to listen to me. You know guys like him, they look at us like we're scenery. Time to change acts? Just move the clowns around a little and bring on the flyers. I was just letting a little air out of his balloon."

"Yeah, you're just the one to do it, aren't you?" Mary turned back and wiped the last maroon smudges from the corners of her eyes.

"Oh, but when you get laughs out of their acts it's all right, is it? I got to put in twenty years before I can ad-lib. That the way it works?"

Mary just looked at me, shaking her head. She stood up and walked across the trailer. "You think I'm making fun of the other performers? That what you think I'm doing?" She stopped by the sofa, staring at me, then put her hand on my shoulder. "I forget how it was first year out. Everybody in the show knowing each other. You work sixteen hours on Saturdays with a couple of clowns, doing board-swings in a carpenter routine with timing like you're inside their brains. And then the show's over. They take off their make-up and go out for a couple of beers and don't know you from Adam."

"Hey, I'm not feeling sorry for myself. I've had my share of drinks with the boys."

"Let me guess. The Too Loose Caboose."

I shrugged.

"So you've heard all the Mary stories," she said, smiling and winking at me. "You come here to get laid?"

"No!"

"Why not? I'm not that old," she said.

"It's not like that," I said. "For one thing, I never heard *those* stories. At least not all the way to the end. No, really, I mean it."

Mary's smile dropped and she looked at me thoughtfully. "Tough luck kid. Those are the best."

"I came here, I don't know, to learn something from you."

Mary laughed again softly. "From me? You want me to tell you about clowns? You want to know what we're supposed to be doing?

Then what are you going to do, write it all down, go home and practice in front of the mirror? Okay, here goes. You ready? Love and Death. That's it. Love and Death are the only two things worth talking about. You want to talk about Death?"

"No."

"Neither do I," she said and sat down to me. She put her arms around me and rolled in with a laugh and a quick hard kiss.

What surprised me wasn't Mary's kiss but what I did. Kissed back. Hard and long.

It wasn't her being older. Hell, I didn't care about that. I liked it. It was feeling so hungry for her. I hadn't felt anything like that just sitting there in her trailer talking. Matter of fact, I was basically sick of sex. I'd picked up girls on the road, lots of them, that's what clowns do. I mean when you're performing you're sexless. There's nothing in the baggy pants but comedy shorts and rubber chickens. But once the make-up's off clowns think they've got something to prove. And I did. But after a while, after all those mornings-after, waking up with a hangover and a stranger, I'd had enough, there was nothing left to prove. I hadn't even thought about sex for the past month. Until now.

I slipped her robe off her shoulders and she slid her arms free, undressing me as we kissed. I expected her to be all knotted muscles, all bruises and scars from twenty years of falls and injuries. But her skin was soft and she felt smooth and strong.

After all the Mary stories, where I had to fill in the endings, I expected something different. I didn't think we'd be hanging from chandeliers or bathing in Crisco, still, I guess I expected something wild from her and kind of held back.

"Come on, honey. You're a big guy. Let yourself go. I'm not going to break," Mary said and lay back on the sofa.

So I pulled her to me and kissed her hard again, opening up her mouth and arms and legs with mine. Everything I did was perfect and Mary responded just right, rolling back on the sofa and fitting her body into mine. I lifted my head and looked across the room into the mirror. There was Mary wrapped around me, head thrown back, clinging to me like I was a piece of shipwreck. Then her eyes opened and I saw her looking at me—watching me watch. She was smiling at me. Like something was all of a sudden so damn funny. I wanted to stop but I couldn't. She was holding me too tight and moving us both with her hips. I tried to push her away but then I was coming and I collapsed on top of her. She pulled me down tight to her and put her lips to my neck, making a soft sound from her throat. A breathy gasp that sounded exactly like Marilyn Monroe. As though she'd rehearsed it. Like an act.

I pulled away from her and just stared in revulsion.

Mary said, "Poor Loverboy. Something go wrong?"

"What was that? What are you, some kind of animal?"

Mary shrugged. "I'm a performer. I perform with performers. I perform for spectators. You're a spectator, Loverboy. You like watching yourself make love. Was it a good show?"

"Me?" I shouted. "At least my acts stay in the ring. You don't know the difference between inside and out. That's sick. You know that? That's real sick."

Mary shoved me away. "Oh, right. Save it for those bastards in the stands. I'm real funny out there dressed like an undertaker, aren't I? What the hell do they think they look like to me? Yeah, do my act and walk out. Suddenly everyone's just lovely. Aren't we all lovely? Yes, it's sick," she said hoarsely. "It makes me sick."

She stalked off to the bathroom and I heard the shower start. I was mad and confused and just wanted the hell out. I dressed quickly and opened the door to leave. Then I heard her laughing. I slammed the trailer door behind me and started back across the field.

Billy came out of the back of the Big Top and spotted me. "Kid! Where you been? Why the long face?" He looked across the field from me to Mary's trailer. "A little heart-to-heart with Mary? Come on. I'll show you where I started out." He turned and started walking toward the midway then spun back, jerking his head for me to follow. I ran after him.

The games were closing down. What was left of the crowd from the show was being herded back out under the archway. We moved toward the sideshow tent. Billy slashed his way through the crowd with his elbows, swearing and threatening murder, and I squeezed in after him, getting hit with the revenge of his victims. The barker at the front of the tent was waving his cane. "Show's over. Let's go. Move it."

Billy shoved his way toward the voice, yelling, "Lip!"

"Legs!"

He and the barker started talking, completely ignoring me. They moved along the edge of the tent, away from the crowd, and I tagged along behind them picking up what I could, pretending I was part of the conversation.

Lennie the Lip was telling Billy there wasn't likely to be another job like this again. This was the last major sideshow in America. "People don't want to look at attractions no more. No, we can't be displaying freaks, it de*means* them. So what are they going to do, join the astronaut program? You take Dolphin Boy, a real wonder of nature. What's he doing? He's in a home in Florida. Fifty-one-years old, he ain't never going to work again. They put the attractions outta work, they close down the sideshows. No sideshows, no place for sword-suckers, snake-wrasslers, or bodybenders to work. Hey, most of the attractions work their asses off here. If they got asses. You got no arms and legs and all you're good for is third base, you better damn well have Maury Wills sliding into you if you want to work New Yankeeland."

I looked around at the "attractions." Aside from the sword-swallower, snake-charmer, and contortionist, there was a bearded-lady doing a lame hula, a monkey-faced man swinging from ropes, an armless man rolling a cigarette with his toes.

The crowd was gone. Lennie and Billy were joined by the rest of the Oldtimers at the front of the tent. I was at the other end, by a series of funhouse mirrors. I walked along looking at my own distorted image. I heard a voice behind me.

"Hey, Loverboy!" Mary walked over, her hair still wrapped in a towel. She put her arm through mine like nothing had happened. "Come on. I want you to meet someone."

I started to yank my arm away and Mary said, "No, no, no. We don't want to look rude in front of your friends, do we?"

I looked back at the Oldtimers who were smiling and watching me. I didn't say anything. I was too angry. I just watched our reflections bend as we walked along until we came to the last mirror. There was a guy just sitting in a chair, staring at the mirror.

Mary said, "Loverboy, meet John, the Funhouse Man. John, Loverboy. Loverboy's a First-of-May in the Big Show."

The man didn't say anything, didn't move.

He was rail-thin, his body was hunchbacked and twisted, with long fingers bent nearly horizontal from his hand. He looked as though just being alive was an act of pain but his face was normal and fixed in a smile. His eyes never moved off the mirror in front of him. I stared a moment at him and then followed his look. In the mirror, I was a twisted, bent monster standing next to the perfectly corrected figure of the Funhouse Man. His reflected expression was a surprised and horrified leer.

Mary leaned close and whispered, "Think you can learn to do that?" Then she laughed again. Behind me, the Oldtimers were watching and laughing, and from in front of me came a squeaking hissing laugh from the Funhouse Man.

Now I'm not saying I learned anything right away from Mary, except maybe to use a little precaution and a little protection. The only burning truth I got from her in the next three days was a burning dribbling truth that came from my crotch.

I went back to see Mary. Not to apologize, not to thank her for her setting me straight. I went back ready to shove my groin out at her and point an accusing finger.

The morning of our New York City opening, I stole Jonesy's van, drove it three hours back to that little town in Massachusetts, and totaled his shocks. When I arrived at the site, the circus was gone. I threw open the door and got out, staring around at the empty space and the pines. In the meadow where the tents once stood, there were were only three circles of dying yellow grass.

*The sage, Chuang Tzu, dreamt one night that he was
a butterfly dreaming he was a man, and when he woke
he did not know whether he was a man who dreamt he
was a butterfly or a butterfly dreaming he was a man.*

Notes from the
Belly of the Whale

You are crossing the reassuring and pitiless monotony of prairie—
a xerox of corn and wheat and corn. From the comfort of airplanes it
has always seemed a flat quilt of farm, a sanguine breadth of cornucopia
between the mountains, between the living flaps of the nation. But here
at ground level, the landscape is not ever truly flat but rolling, mutable
with hypnotic undulation—a swell of hill, a vista of infinity that is lost
again as you descend into the hollow of the next rise.

You pass a sign: Logical Junction Ahead—and see a series of signs
stretching along the roadside preceding you and imagine they will read:
Logical Junction, 1 mile; Logical Junction, 1/2 mile; Logical Junction,
1/4 mile; Logical Junction, 1/8 mile; Logical Junction, 1/16 mile. . . .

But at the first sign you laugh. It bears the reassuring highway
doggerel of your youth:

*Beyond the hill, the road divides
Which way to go you must decide.
Two men stand there beneath the rise.
One tells the truth, the other lies
To one a question you may pose
You'll be answered by the one you chose
Then pick your road but pick it well—
One road's to Home and one's to Hell.*

If this seems rough, your road you'll pave
With Occam's Razor and...
BURMA SHAVE

You come to the fork in the road. Two dirt-streaked tractors are pulled alongside one another in a shimmer of heat. The men converse with the familiarity born of rural distance—comfortable, laughing, shaking their heads. At your appearance they fall silent, watching the dusty cloud of car approach them. Relax. You know this one. You ask the right question, "If I ask *him* which way is the correct road to the village will he tell me this one?" "This one" is how you put it, the question posed, a finger aimed, at random. It is pure and simple. One road gives a yes; the other a no. The purity. The simplicity. It's astounding. It has nothing to do with either man or road. Any creature, any road would serve. Just the words themselves hold all the answers. You feel an almost visceral pleasure, the click of logic opening hormonal floodgates in your brain, blood coursing thickly in celebration, delivering congratulations to your muscles. You have brought me this far, I have delivered you a path. Brain and brawn dance with energy again.

You wave, unnoticed. The men have already resumed their conversation. You dial vainly for a radio station, press the accelerator toward where the new road disappears beyond the next rise.

Somewhere, like a mattress pea, you wonder:

The man who answers the question, did he really know what the other man was going to say?

A small dead thing. Grey, furry dead thing. It's a whatchamacallit. . . . Too late. Gone.

When I was just starting to write, I decided to rewrite, in first person, the story of Jonah from the Bible. I loved the stance of the man. The man, not the prophet. His refusal to prophesy. His denial of fate. In my story, I wrote easily, with gut recognition, a rich, bawdy account of his encounter with God, his reaction, my reaction, when told to prophesy the fate of Nineveh, Jonah raising a central finger to the Almighty, booking passage on a ship for Tarshish. On board the ship, while engaged in a poker game with the ship's crew, Jonah, me, recognizes the sailors from *Moby Dick* (fictional time was at my youthful mercy) and they recognize him. They throw him overboard into the roiling sea where the Leviathan, his gleaming albino symbolism bedecked with the screaming Ahab, swallows me.

I was in the whale's belly. I can remember seeing it, an immense Gothic dome, lit with iron lanterns. The whale's ribs formed two massive palindromic staircases that disappeared into a charcoal-grey darkness beyond the flickering rims of lamp light. I stood in this cathedral on the thick, rubbery-wet floor of the whale's stomach lining, counter-balancing the undulations of the floor and the waves of swallowed minnows that splashed against my ankles.

I remember remembering something while writing this. A newspaper article about a real-life Jonah. A dead whale washed up on the shores of some Greek island. A village boy had run to gather the entire town, swearing that the dead monster spoke to him, cried out for help. When the astounded townspeople heard the voice themselves there had been a moment when they all sank to their knees in awe, in a mass astonishment at this miracle, until the voice began to swear at them in the unmistakeable accents of a Greek merchant seaman. When they cut him out, frantic finally to slash the blubber prison, the sailor was blind and naked and his skin and hair had been bleached white by the acids in the stomach. Like a fish born in an underground river. I remember remembering that. And I remember then thinking that, in the Biblical story, the whale's belly is where Jonah is suddenly converted back to righteousness. Where he caves in, at last, to God's assignment.

In the vaporous acid mist of the whale's belly I set off on one of the staircases, curving upward into the murkiness until I was walking in total darkness, a profound noncolour that intimated to me my own invisibility, bumping the toes of my bare feet on each successive rib, my right hand against the rubbery-smooth wall of whalegut for balance. I walked with my head tilted back, certain that these stairs must some-how end at the whale's blowhole, straining to make out a small circle of light. When I saw the light above me I felt a smugness, satisfaction at my innate comprehension of whale-innard navigation. As I approached, the circle grew lighter and larger, finally stretching to impossible dimensions. I entered the rim of flickering light and I found myself back in the cathedral of the belly walking up the other staircase, the one I had not chosen, still walking up, though inverted, like an Escher etching. I felt then the full weight of Despair, the capitalized form, felt its capitalization settle on and encompass me like an institution.

What I felt was the Despair of Jonah. I did not even know of the Despair of God.

Though I have returned again and again to the file in my study that holds the now-petrifying pages of my Jonah story, I have never finished the story. I am trapped to this day in the whale's belly.

You come to the fork in the road. The road splits wide. Arcs of 120 degrees separate each road. Trails of dust approach you as you approach the hub. Two other travellers simultaneously converge upon the same spot. You stop, they stop. There is excessive eye-blinking, head-turning, whatever the necessary signs are for general stupefaction. When you speak it is not the congruity of the words but the purity of the three-part harmony that astonishes you.

Something that seeps in through the vent, some gas, a secret an entire city must lift one cheek to loose, steel being born, old pig blood, shame. It belongs here. We're gone.

David lies flat on the carpet of my study. He is whispering into his Fisher-Price cassette player.

"David, please, I can't concentrate when you're whispering like that."

He looks up at me. "I'm writing a story," he says.

I smile, thinking I never thought it would be me he would want to grow up to be. "Me too," I say.

"I know," he says. "That's in my story. You're writing a story about me." David stops, looks vacantly at me, thinking about this. Then he laughs. "Isn't that funny?"

"Not funny, exactly," I say, searching for the right word. "Clever. I guess it's clever."

David shakes his head. "No, it's funny."

This path has a vague familiarity. The road is soft with African dust. The vague yellow left by the billion crumbled pages of every edition extant of *Little Black Sambo*, recalled to Africa, dumped unmercifully here to erode. The yellow of tiger-butter. The men are skeletal, ebony, seven-foot towers of permanence, in leopard skins, clutching spears and long ovals of skin-wrapped shields. There is such heat, a sun that centres itself in the universe above the bump in your pith helmet, a sun with a mission to sear your pith, helmet or no.

You are blessed by the hopelessness of your mission. It has torn from you every science that guided you this far. Into this dust, below this sun. You leave behind trails of compasses, maps, Richard Burton volumes, mini-cassettes of the tribal voices like dreamscapes by which you sought to orient yourself (when he says "beyond the sleeping dragon lies a river of gold" he means. . .). You are truly and blessedly broken by heat, dust clogs every instrument and reduces it to weight, all your science crushed at last by thirst. You become animal again, your nostrils able to flare at the scent of water. And you have rushed forward along the road, your past shed and lost in the yellow dust cloud that trails you. Utterly at the mercy of thirst and sun. You come to the fork in the road.

A thumb. A long and delicate thumb. A thumb that moves with a certainty of desire, motion of wrist along the thick root, the wrinkle of thumb knuckle, across the flat plane of translucent horn. It nails its direction to the wind. Gone.

I watch TV, a contemptible confession for a writer to make. Cop shows, mystery shows, even an occasional sitcom. The lure of this low art is the same—the characters seem to arrive weekly with amnesia. The cop who fell in love with the gold-hearted whore last week (thus condemning her instantly to death) has done all his grieving, allayed his guilt, melted the frost from around his heart and is ready, once again, to sign his death warrant of love. The soap operas, defined by cliché, present full-blown amnesia, brought on by a carcrash, or an emotional shock. It will last a week or so and then another trauma will be written in to cure it. Or they offer the alternate form—the long-lost twin whose true identity must be concealed at all costs, who is adopted without question by the sibling's family and friends.

There is, no doubt, a sickness of soul in the millions of us who watch and suffer this epidemic desire for amnesia, certainly symptomatic of the intolerable ordinariness of everyday life. But imagine it—to arise each morning in a new house, a stranger to yourself, to roll over in bed to an exotic stranger who welcomes you and makes love to you with a wide-eyed smile of wonder and delight, and then to walk out into the alien world again. The allure seems to me undeniable.

Wait. Yes, certainly you have the right question. This is iron logic. Chrome logic. This road, this man, yes. If he answers yes take that road. But. . . . These guys, both of them, why would they think they know you? Their *lederhosen* and goofy, eager grins. What the hell, the damn castle's right there. You can see the damn castle, for God's sake. Titanium logic. Ask the damn question. What had they thought you were? Land surveyor?

A pleasant thought: to drop one's name out the window at very high speeds.

In the midst of the most familiar arguments I begin to calculate. The lives of both my wives have been so sad. This is astonishing to me—this intersection of discontent. Their friends, they have assured me, are not their friends, merely acquaintances, merely companions. I never imagine this to be the case. There has always been the buzz of conversation that lulls at my approach, the sense of intrusion into conspiracy as I walk into a room where my current wife is speaking to her friend. I have no desire to eavesdrop on these conversations but wish, instead, merely to witness it, the radiance of the laughter between women, the secretive luminous glow of women in confession.

I married my first wife, Arleen, right after high school. We both entered the same university, worked and studied together, claimed the same goals, formed the same friendships. After our wedding, Arleen saved the husband-wife figures off our wedding cake and had them encased in a clear lucite cube, his right hand fingertipped to her left, both clear-eyed gazing ahead. After university and law school, we applied to the same law firms and were told that it would be impossible to work together—that married associates just carried too much "emotional baggage" between them, that the personal would pollute the professional.

There began the slow warp of our lives. Our circle of friends became two circles, our mutual reliance became mutual independence. At night, when we both enclosed the remnants of our work in our briefcases, when we slipped into bed surrounded with our separate worlds of woes, Arleen would turn to me and begin a recitation of discontents. There were holes in her soul, there was a routeless path she walked, she was so alone and so different than all the other people in her office. I thought she was asking for my help and I listened and pounded at the problems with the power of logic, trying to hammer circum- stances into solutions. I would offer my solutions, mere suggestions, and Arleen would glare at me and turn furiously away. I felt a welling up of impotent rage, drilled bitter stares into the knotted muscles of her back. I would reach out toward her, my hands rigid claws of frustration, softening at the touch of her skin into a strong, soothing massage.

As we repeated this scene nightly, I quit working on solutions to her anxieties, nodding and listening while Arleen's words slid past me. I found myself thinking of numbers, random numbers, computing the square roots of three- four- five-digit numbers in my head while Arleen spoke. She seemed more content with me, the preoccupation and careful consideration I seemed to have with her problems. She would finish talking and reach out for me and I would hold her quietly until I had rechecked the calculations in my head. Then we would make love. This went on for another year before she announced, one night, that her firm wanted her to transfer to Toronto. I continued to compute roots, six digits extracted to six decimal places, holding her while she began to sketch out the legalities of a divorce.

After my divorce from Arleen I looked at the legacy of our lives together and couldn't garner even the slightest clue. We were true lawyers—there was no room in retrospect for innocence, just guilt or nonguilt. And when we looked at that life we acted as our own jury— agreed on the verdicts. But that's unfair of us—never to be able to claim innocence. I certainly appeared not guilty—how could I not? Didn't I humbly step aside to allow Arleen her career? And as her jury, in the face our parents and friends, I have always announced her as not guilty, letting them see me sweetly tortured by the verdict. But here is the truth: I claim Arleen is truly innocent; proclaim my guilt. I know now and believe I knew then the crimes I committed in that marriage. The desire to manoeuvre her, the silent calculations I performed while hearing the testimonies of her discontent. I was letting the facts pile up in my favour. I could stand aside and let her dismantle the remnant of a marriage in ruins, allowing everyone to see only my tight-lipped anguish at the demolition and not the cold, calculating complicity of my silence as our marriage rotted from inside our conjugal bed.

There are the ropes, like bell-pulls, soft golden velvet tapering to luxurious chocolate brown tufts. They twitch and sway in the wind, as though they were alive, as though they both invited your touch. Beneath them the road divides and disappears behind two monumental black screens. Pull the cord, reveal the road.

You hear the harmony of muted purrs. The resonance of desire in a satin throat; the bass, a distant thunder of feline hunger. They fuse in the warm summer air, the indistinct light of dusk, and give no clue as to which rope reveals which.

There, was it a trick of imagination? No, there, the soft murmuring laugh and the tiniest shiver to the right. Yes. You pull and the screen rises. My god, what is this beast?

It is monstrous. The sunken eyes of Shelley, the wide expanse of Einstein's forehead, Virginia Woolf's damp and flowing hair, the glistening teeth of DeQuincy, its crimson-wet and open chest displays two hearts, Blake and Heisenberg, corkscrewing arrhythmically into each other, the ghost soul of Poe, the balls of Frost, the haunches of Marilyn Monroe, and, still writhing in your hand, the tail, tolled by an idiot.

He is crouched at the side of the road, sitting on his cracked and sticker-adorned leather suitcase, hunched twist-necked over a strip of paper, his delicate thumb crooked over a cheap institutional pen, writing. At the car roar he raises his head but does not seem to focus on the car, looking, rather, inward at some hidden movie screen of memory. His eyes do not follow the car as it dopplers past. Gone.

I had thought that the strange displacement into calculation, my absorption into mathematics, was somehow a function of the cold logical progression of my life with Arleen, could never happen in my relations with my second wife.

Jordan is a dancer and a choreographer. On stage, she is brilliant, bending emotion and philosophy into lithe, muscular motion. We met on a tour of the U.S. Southwest, watching a Hopi corn dance performed for a convergence of bus tours. Jordan had seen the dancers before and was, instead, watching the crowd watch the dancers. I was aware of the impossibility of really seeing the dance. The dance was not in any sense expression, it was spectacle, meant to be seen by tourists, so layered with the sense of being watched that the actual dance barely existed. The dancers seemed coated with the sense of display, their movements leaden and ironic. When I began to watch the crowd, I could see the thick layers of spectacle that surrounded us and when I saw Jordan, watching, as I was, the watching, the filmy web seemed to evaporate. Unconsciously, she assumed the stance and expression of everyone she watched. Then she turned toward me. Busted, I shrugged and she laughed. We understood instantly our complicity. We slipped to the back of the crowd but when I moved over to introduce myself Jordan was gone. I caught sight of her climbing into a tour bus and followed.

"Hello?"

"Ssshhh!" she hissed. I went up the stairs and found her seated next to the sleeping figure of a small boy. "I'm Jordan," she whispered, "this is David."

I introduced myself for the first time as a writer who used to be a lawyer—as though the future had already arrived. David woke, startled, at the sight of me then snuggled into his mother and went back to sleep.

Jordan and I talked with instant familiarity. The bus left, it wasn't my bus but I stayed on. I never found out where my luggage ended up. Jordan and David and I left the tour at Taos. We spent another ten days in deserts. We talked about what deserts meant, how necessary they were, how they were the only places left whose reality had not been toured away. We talked earnestly and practically about the future. They lived in Seattle and I romanced them by phone and shuttle for the next three months. We married. I left my job, sold everything, surprised to find myself suddenly rich, and moved to Seattle. I felt certain that from the moment we caught sight of our secret spying at the corn dance, no conversation between us could be without the ozone crackle of clarity.

This marriage, I vowed, would be different. No deceit of silence. And my writing, too, I swore, would be a hammering of the soul until the devils of self-deceit flung themselves onto the page begging for the mercy of the compassionate shades that read my stories.

This morning as we woke, Jordan turned to me and said, "I dreamed of Vlado." David's father. "I dreamed he was auditioning for me and that he danced a dance about me. He was singing while he danced. I couldn't understand the words but they made me cry because I knew that they were supposed to be my words. It was such a lonely song. I came to the stage to stop him, to tell him I couldn't use him in the piece but then we were dancing together, then naked, then making love. 'What was I saying?' I kept asking him. 'What were the words to the song?' He kept looking over my shoulder and I looked behind me. You were standing there with your arm around David's shoulder and you were watching us. Vlado said, 'They are his words.' I think he meant you." Jordan stopped. "Do you hate me for my dream?"

"No, of course not," I said, holding her. We lay that way until David knocked on the door.

"Mom," he called. "I ate breakfast and I made my own lunch."

We bolted from bed. The kitchen was a disaster of cereal boxes, dirty knives, plastic wrap. David's school clothes were covered with peanut butter and jam. We beamed and praised his independence. I cleaned up the mess as Jordan washed him and supervised his clothes-changing. We walked him to the bus together, trying to stifle our delight, protect his dignity. After a final wave to the disappearing bus, we collapsed with laughter, the dream forgotten.

Tonight we've argued over nothing, both of us irritable at the current failure of our work. Jordan worked on her platform at the far end of the loft, trying to recreate her dream. In the corner of my eye I could see her motions swirl then jerk angrily to a stop. In the corner of her eye she must have seen me—pounding on the keyboard, halting, laying my head down across my folded arms, rising and pacing—trying to explain myself to you. I never mentioned my problems to her. Jordan is filled to overflowing with her own frustrations: her vague discontent with the piece she's choreographing, the medium of dance itself, and the walls between desire and expression. I choked back the urge to supply her with solutions.

Our workspace is not ideal—we would both prefer to work in solitude, unobserved—but we agree that to wall off the loft would make us claustrophobic. Several times tonight, Jordan caught my glance, the dip of my head as I turned away, and at last called out, "You're writing about me again."

"No, I'm not," I protested. "I never write about you." I tried again to explain how writers create jigsaw worlds from scraps of fact but she dismissed my words.

"What am I in this one? The bitch or the love goddess?"

Jordan sleeps now, her dream-mind sealed from me, her body arcing in some purposeful pose.

And I find myself at 2 A.M. rechecking, to six decimal places, the square root of a six-digit number I extracted even while making love to her.

At the fork in the road you stop, overwhelmed with *déjà vu*. Have you been here before? The tired thump of your heart roots you to these crossroads. Is this the same fork, the same men? Certainly there have been forks along the way, hundreds of these decisions have propelled you this far. Yet when you turn and look back you see only a straight flat boulevard of history. The inevitability of retrospect. You have the urge to quit—to suspend time by refusing to choose. That is, of course, a choice itself.

The headlights catch in the eyes of something. Almond shaped gleaming emeralds. Eyes that reflect without recognition. Something like a film of memory dulls the glow. Then they're gone.

In the dream, something has gone wrong with the regulator in my brain—that weighing device that sorts white noise into sense. A glancing blow from a wildly thrown toy has knocked it out and everything suddenly carries the same authority. Weather reports, computer hum, borborygmae, car drone, paper crackle, food slurps, all enter and receive equal consideration, equal value. I pulp sound to light, smell to touch, taste to the drying shores of unconscious seas. I walk about the house flooded with sense, stiff-legged, Frankenstein's monster, arms outstretched, finger-wriggling, nostrils flaring, my tongue darting to taste the air like a lizard. Careen over David's toys, cautious of crushing carpet nap, Jordan, dust mites. I am panicked and arrive with my family in the emergency room. Though I hear my name called, I don't understand how to respond to it. I have to be dragged by Arleen to the reception desk. I am asked to state my problem. The air is frigid and puffs of vapour stream out my nostrils. I jaw clouds of anguish, don't know what kind of doctor to ask for. Point to my head. I am given a psychic map of my brain and I am ashamed to say I can't find my regulator.

Both signposts point the same way. Which to follow? Where are you going, silly? What is it you want? Contrariwise, there isn't much point deciding until the road divides.

There's a sign up ahead. A great big picture of a fork. Two figures stand below it. Dressed in bright pink and chartreuse-striped blazers, short green pants buttoned tight over drum-taut belly pots, yellow beanies, bright yellow shoes, they stand beneath the big fork sign, heels together, the toes of their lemon shoes splayed, rocking like two indecisive bowling pins. They look like nothing more than large blow-up Rock 'em, Sock 'em dolls.

"If y'think we're here to be gewgawed at," says First Boy, "we're not. Nohow."

"Contrariwise, if y'plan on gewgawing you're going to have to pay," says Next Boy. "And how."

"I'm so sorry," you say.

"NOT!" they shout, and the very wind of their words puffs them back on their heels. They bobble, bop shoulders, boing little pot-bellies, slowly come to rest.

Now which is Dum and which is Dee? They *must* be labelled on the back, you think. If they'd just spin a bit more when they bobble I'm sure I could see. It is so tiresome to not be able to address them properly. I am certain they know the way out of here, if only I knew the right way to ask them. And then there's the battle. They've got to agree to fight.

"It isn't so, nohow," says First Boy.

"Contrariwise," says Next Boy, "if it was so, it might be; and if it were so, it would be; but as it isn't, it ain't. That's logic."

The roar you hear might be the monstrous crow.

"NOT!" they shout gleefully. "It's him!"

You see me underneath a tree. I'm tossing and turning, snoring and groaning with anguish. You bend beside me, your hand extended softly above me as though to comfort the atmosphere. You think, what can he be dreaming about?

"Why about you!" says First Boy.

"And where d'ye think you'd be if he were to leave off dreaming?" says Next Boy. "Why nowhere. You're just a sort of thing in his dream!"

"Shh," you whisper, "you'll wake him."

"Shh," they chorus softly. "Shhhh. Shhhh. Shhhh."

The hushed sounds reach inside you, loosen your limbs, tug leadenly at your eyelids and you curl beside me and sleep.

A mist of rain swept off by the wipers. We navigate almost blindly through the murk. The lights flash at the chain across the road. I hit the brakes and we squeal, fish-tailing to a stop.

"It's him. It's the same hitchhiker," you say.

He stands there holding one end of the chain, the other end disappears on the opposite side of the road, tied to something lost in the charcoal blackness. The headlights illuminate a pile of bloody roadkill by his cracked and patched luggage. Something smells of decay.

"Let's pick him up," you whisper. "It's raining."

"No," I tell you. "He looks weird. He might be dangerous. He's just standing there, not hitching. We don't even know if he's going our way."

You look at me, almost laughing. "You made him. Make him safe."

"No, no. He's not one of mine. He stands outside of us, don't you see?"

You laugh.

"That's the truth!" I insist.

"He's the Truth?"

You are still laughing when I ease the car forward. The chain is made of paper links, already dissolving in the rain.

It's been such a long journey. This is the easiest part. Let me ask them. I know the right answer. I know, and we're so tired, and logic is my language. I can crack their skulls with the cold embrace of rationality. I can extract truth from them with all the gleaming sharp devices of inquisition. I turn from you, they turn toward me. We face each other, gunslinger-style, spitting precision instruments, fingers twitching at the ready. "Count!" I tell you, "Backwards from three."

"Count!" they say.

We are a triangle of cruel smiles.

You open your mouth and orchids spill out.

The car rolls through the chain, lights piercing through the darkness. A strip of paper sticks in the wipers. I stop the wipers and you reach out your window, pluck the paper from the upright wiper. A long wide strip, twisted a half-turn with its ends glued together, the print curves from outside to inside and again back outside. You arc your neck following the print as you read aloud:

In 1796, a Chinese monk was invited to leave his country for the first time to attend a conference on natural history in France. His host, a Catholic priest and an avid lepidopterist, delighted in exhibiting to the monk his collection of rare species, meticulously mounted, labelled, and displayed in neat rows of glass cases. The monk viewed the specimens slowly and deliberately. When reaching the end of the collection, the monk turned his gaze upon a huge crucifix mounted on the priest's wall, giving it the same considerate and careful attention. After watching the monk for a few minutes, the priest moved next to him and asked softly, "Do you know what that is?"

The monk nodded and replied, "Yes. It is Chuang Tzu finding out the hard way."

The headlights blink out. We travel in darkness, unsure even of our speed, relying on the monotony of prairie highway. The first light from behind us tints the landscape, outlines in blood the indistinct shapes, then washes clean to grey. Only now can we judge our speed in the blur of the white lines that climb before us. Over the next rise the dawn illuminates the next fork, the hitchhiker alone at the fork, surrounded by his roadkill, his suitcase, his books. I lift my foot from the gas. I feel the press of your hand on mine and I lift it from the wheel.

Things scatter as we aim for the Truth.

(*for D.D.M.*)

David and Goliath

David is being bad again. Up in his room, perched on his bed, clutching his blanket. Bad again. Screaming and screaming.

I take my arms from around his and begin, in a soothing voice, to interrupt his screams. I am unsure whether it is what I say or how I sound that quiets him. We are, in the end, locked in a hug. Father to son, the male pietà—David slumps in my arms as though slain by my words. His lower lip protrudes in his obstinate pout as he shakes his head against the relentless pounding of my voice.

"Don't say that," David commands.

What?

"Don't say anything," David warns.

I won't.

"Stop talking." His voice edges toward tremolo.

I leave the room. He is to sit and think about what he's done. Coloured the carpet, terrorized the cat, knocked down the baby. David is being bad again.

David must never be told that he is bad. Only what David is doing is bad. Painting with food, flooding the bathroom, scissoring sheets into sports-patterned ghosts. Do's and don'ts too numerous to fit onto the star-covered charts I made that hang on the bathroom door. Thou shalt not touch the baby's face. Thou shalt pick up thy toys. The path to David's heaven is paved with shiny gold gum-backed stars.

I sit in the chair outside David's room while he talks to his blanket.

"I don't like to be here all by myself."

Behind my closed eyes, the sounds of the words twist themselves into pictures. Pictures of David's mouth. Silently, I mouth the words I used to say before I learned to leave the room. "You're not supposed to like it," I intone. "You're supposed to think."

"I'm not talking to you," he says.

The baby is blessedly silent. He has slept throughout the exchange. When awake, he seems to respond to David's cry like a hound to a trumpet note, raising his chubby chins and howling. But he can sleep through even the loudest screams. Who knows what dreams they produce in his loyal brain?

Three months ago, snow ringed the backyard in crusty shelves. The midday warmth and the freezing nights had left the snow banks smooth and sculpted into a series of static ocean waves. David had refused his nap. He had the beginnings of the flu. His eyes were red and watery, his cheeks flushed. He'd whined all morning and through lunch. The constant complaints gradually evaporated my initial sympathy for him and I was taking deep breaths to control myself.

At naptime David refused everything. His favourite stuffed animals lay strewn about his bedroom, books were pulled down off the shelves, and even his blanket, his constant source of comfort, was jammed under the bed. He ran from the bedroom to his playroom and refused to be coaxed back to bed. I promised him stories and songs but he held his hands over his ears resisting all offers. At last I picked him up, his legs flailing. I threw him over my shoulder and carried him to his bedroom, dropped him onto his bed and left, slamming the door behind me. I pounded down the stairs and out into the backyard. I stamped into a snow drift, leaving a deep footprint in the icy crystals. For weeks after, whenever I went out to the backyard, the imprint on the snowbank reminded me of David's look of fear and helplessness. I couldn't bring myself to destroy the drift. It was as if only the warming of spring could erase the memory.

"David?" I call softly.

"Chsh, chsh, chsh." He is shooting me with his finger through the closed door, a trick he learned from Arnold, a neighbourhood friend. When Arnold first came over he would take David's toys and shoot him with a cocked finger. It drove David crazy. He would launch himself at Arnold, kicking and shouting and biting, and I would separate them, sending David to his room.

Sometime last month I heard Arnold's "chsh, chsh, chsh" behind me. I turned and watched David face the pointing finger. His mouth fell open, he arched his eyebrows in surprise, knit them in anger, settled them in solution. I remember how proud I was when his finger cocked and the air was doubled with boyish spittle. Chsh, chsh, chsh, chsh, chsh, chsh.

When Arnold misbehaves he must be punished, too. What else can I do and still be honest with David? Arnold's cry is a barely audible squeal. His mouth opens cavernously but only the tiniest mouse-like squeak emerges. Perhaps he cries in registers beyond the human range of hearing. His mother has never come for him when he was sitting squeaking in his chair in the corner. I don't know what I'd tell her. Were the situation reversed, I'd be furious.

David's moral instruction is my province. Listening to my wife's criticisms of David knots the muscles of my neck and shoulders. We used to laugh when we'd agreed on my role as homemaker at the vision of me threatening, "Wait 'til your mother gets home." At first, I couldn't resist interfering every time she disciplined him. I've learned to grip my thighs, watch the baby, or rewash dishes to prevent myself from climbing the stairs. Her anger with David is sometimes explosive. It's easy to forget what a tiny chunk of life his three years are. She'll sometimes stamp down the steps, whisk the baby from my arms, and tell me with a withering voice "He wants *you*." I go slowly up the stairs and impose exactly the same punishment his mother had begun. If David's cries sometimes turn to, "I want my Mommy," I've learned to grit my teeth and ignore them.

Last week the baby crawled toward me looking like a scene from *Night of the Living Dead*. A triangle of blood mixed with baby spit dribbled down his chin forming a goatee of gore. With each wail the triangle lengthened. I swept him up in my arms, soaking up his cries and blood in the soft flannel of my shirt.

"David! What happened?"

"We were being happy."

A tiny line of bright blood showed on the inside of the baby's lower lip.

"He's screaming and bleeding. What did you do?"

"We were playing helicopter. You put your arms out and brrr . . . brrr. . . . David was spinning around the living room. Spinning wildly around, then crashing into the coffee table. "That's what he did."

"Stop it, David. You'll hurt yourself."

"No I won't. See? I'm happy."

"He can't spin around like that. He can barely walk, David. You were spinning him, weren't you? He's not a toy."

"He likes it when I spin him. We were being happy. You just go like this, Daddy. Brrr. . .brrr. . . .

"I know how to turn around, thank you. Don't do it to the baby."

"Mommy says you don't."

"Mommy says I don't know how to spin?"

"Mommy says you don't know how to be happy. You just go like this. Brrr. . .brrr. . .brr."

We have never hit David, although he has been thoroughly pummelled by Arnold. When his mother told him that he would be spanked if he did not stop touching the baby's eyes, David had no idea what she was talking about. I listened from the kitchen as she explained what a spanking was. David laughed and laughed, refusing to believe her.

He witnessed his first spanking last week at the mall. A little girl was howling and had gone limp in the middle of Sears. The child refused to take another step. Her exhausted mother lifted the child over her knee and began to swat her. Before I could stop him, David had rushed over yelling furiously, "No hitting. You stop hitting." I ran to him, feeling the stares of every shopper. I put one hand on his shoulder to calm him and with the other picked up the woman's shopping bags. "You look like you've had a rough day," I said. "Can I help?"

"Mind your own damn business," she snapped, grabbing the bags back from me. Her child stood up, sniffling back tears and running a snot-stiffened sleeve across her face. They left the store without a backward glance.

"Thank you," the manager told me.

"Don't thank me. Thank my son."

She smiled and bent over David. "Thank you."

"You're welcome," he said.

*   *   *

It's David's belief that all such human clashes can be resolved immediately, with his intervention and a word from Daddy. Once, while David and I were watching the end of a ball game on TV, the baby awoke screaming in the midafternoon heat. I rushed to change him while David pitched imaginary fastballs past George Bell. The baby was cleaned and diapered and fed and held, struggling in vain against his heavy eyelids, when David began shouting in the living room. With the baby squealing harmony, I ran to David who was crying, pointing at the screen and shouting, "You stop hitting." The baseball game had ended and been replaced by boxing on the all-sports network. I switched it off then tried to explain boxing to David. No matter what I said, the very idea seemed absurd and David didn't care anyway. Hadn't I stopped the fight?

When my wife and I argued again at breakfast (why didn't we ever go anywhere, who *cares* if the stove was filthy, why do we have to trim the baby's fingernails every week—he hates it), David intervened. He stood up on his chair and screamed. I ignored him. (Of course she didn't care how dirty the stove was—she never cooked, how nice of her to notice the baby *had* fingernails when she hadn't even noticed his new teeth.) The baby joined the chorus, surprising us to silence.

"Be quiet, David."

"You be quiet. You stop making Mommy mad."

Mommy rose from the table and ran out the door. Slam. She didn't come home last night.

I open the door to David's room. He is holding his blanket, whispering to a tattered stuffed animal, "I want my Mommy."

"I want your Mommy too."

"I'm not talking to you," he tells me, clinging to his blanket.

The doorbell rings, waking the baby into a sudden bout of wailing. I gather the baby out of his crib, hike with him on my hip to the door. I open the door and feel the clear crisp sun- powered air rush in around me. It is Mrs. Ross and Arnold. "I'm sorry. Did I wake the baby?" she asks, chucking the baby under his chins.

I sigh.

"You look like you've had a rough day. Why don't I take the boys to the park? I'd take the baby, but I think he's hungry. Aren't you hungry?" The baby clings to me, burying his face in my chest.

Mrs. Ross has come to save my life. I repress the urge to scream at her, to bury my fist in the soft folds of her stomach. Instead, I ask her to wait a moment and go back upstairs.

David is sitting at the top of the stairs, holding his blanket and crooning softly to himself. I sit down next to him, balancing the baby on my hip.

"Make Mommy come home."

"David, I can't make her come home. Why don't you go to the park with Arnold and Mrs. Ross, and Mommy will probably be home for dinner."

"You make Mommy come home." He dumps his blanket in my lap and brushes past me down the stairs and out the front door.

"I'll have him back by five," calls Mrs. Ross.

I sit at the top of the stairs feeling the comfortable softness of the blanket, redolent with the scent of David. Above me hangs a photograph taken six months ago of him wearing my shoes, standing before a mirror. He is smiling at his own image dwarfed by my shoes. Holding his blanket, I feel shrunk to my son's size. I don't know where my wife is. I don't know if she'll come home. I feel I have to fill shoes impossibly big.

The baby refuses his bottle. His diapers are dry. He has no fever. His nails are trimmed. He is cutting no new teeth. He has no rashes, no insect bites, no allergies, no hidden bruises.

He is screaming at the top of his lungs.

I gently lay him down in his crib. The mobile above him plays "Brahm's Lullaby" but can barely be heard over the din.

I pour myself a drink and walk down the hall. In my room, slumped on my bed, clutching my bourbon, I join the baby. Crying and crying.

And then I just stop. I get up. I carry the untasted bourbon into the kitchen and dump it in the sink. The rich oaky fumes almost nauseate me.

I go to the baby's room. He's still crying. "Hey, Joe. Joe-Joe. Daddy's here." He looks at me with curiosity. He's forgotten why he's crying but continues as though it was an obligation. "Come on, Big Joe. Let's go get David."

His eyes widen at the mention of David's name. He cries as I pick him up but now I imagine it's because David's not here. As soon as we step outside, he's quiet. "That's right, Joe-Joe. We're going to get David."

Halfway to the park I stop. There's something I've forgotten. I stand still on the sidewalk waiting to remember. I haven't left a note for my wife. What if she comes home?

We look ahead to the park, where the boys are screaming and swinging and Mrs. Ross throws her fat arms up in mock frustration. When I turn towards the house, the baby looks back at me. His face contorts, his lower lip quivers. I lift him onto my shoulders turning, so he can see his brother, and he clenches his fists tightly in my hair. I turn again toward home. There's a shout behind me, "Daddy!" and I twist back away from the house to watch David. He leans out from the swing, holding on with one hand, waving the other at me. I return the wave before heading back toward the house. When I turn, I hear the wet gurgle of Joe-Joe's laugh. I pivot again slowly, then faster and faster, David and the park and the house now just a blur. Brrr...brrr...brrr. I spin with the baby perched on my shoulders, clutching me tightly. Laughing and laughing.

(*for R.D.S. and A.C.S.*)

A Clown's Clown

Clowns are pegs, used to hang circuses on.

P.T. BARNUM

Circuses are pegs from which clowns hang themselves.

FROM *PSYCHOPATHOLOGY AND SLAPSTICK*

Who's that man with the scarf stuck to him?

Stuck to his hand?

Yes.

What's he doing?

Trying to shake it off, I suppose.

And?

It's off his hand. . . .

And stuck to his clothes?

Yes.

Bust my gut.

Sorry?

Steal my breath.

Eh?

I can't look. I'd laugh to death. Whew! Clown can go crazy with a fella like him. Deep breath. Settle down.

That's. . . ?

Stumpy Columbo, clown to clowns.

That's *him*?

You sound incredulous. Say, mind me asking you a question, Boss? You a member of the Fifth Estate?

No.

A Psych Professor from up there at State?

Yes! Perhaps you've read my work. *Psychopathology and Slapstick?* Damn! I messed that one up but good. Struck my paydirt before I should. Pardon, Doc. Gotta punch the clock. Hey Stumpy! How's about a couple lessons? C'mere and show me how to work these questions.

Direct your attention if you will to the little man with the scarf now stuck to his rump. At the sound of his name, he stops whirling around and stumbles across the room, a bag of bones in a cloud of dust, a man whose misery cracks your heart like an eggshell. He strides down the centre of clown alley, blithely tromping through the foam rubber props that litter the floor while clowns peel away in fits of convulsive laughter.

Well, Doc, shall we run it again? Want I should start or'll you begin? I don't know what you. . . .

Stump, I'm rolling, the rhythm's fine. He does his lines and I do mine. So I figure he's a local clown just up to crowd the scene and I start right into the Who-Are-You Routine. Well, the first question's fine, the bit is going great, but the second question bombs. He *does* teach up at State.

That's right. You see, I'm here to invite you. . . .

'Scuse us, Doc, but Stumpy here is cooking. Yes he is, Stump, but how'd you tell just looking? Yeah, blue socks, brown shoes, tweed with leather elbow patches, frayed yellow shirt collar, and nothing quite matches. Deadperfect. I tell you, Doc, Stump'll find a man out deeper than he knows himself. And just look at that puss. Oh mercy. Shatter my kneecaps with slaps. Yessir, a clown's clown. Break your heart like a pressed rose petal. Doc, Stumpy. Stumpy, Doc.

I'm honoured, Mr. Columbo.

Mr. Columbo. . . .

A gale of laughter, bumps and thuds as clowns roll off their stools and onto the floor, clutching their sides, wincing with breathlessness.

Doc rolls a nervous eye, whispers:

Mr. . . . er. . .Stumpy. It would be a great honour for us if you could visit my classes at the university to demonstrate just what exactly forms the Core of Comedy.

A gust of exhaled guffaws sweeps dust down clown alley and wraps around Stumpy. He smiles weakly, his eyes widening as he rocks up onto his toes and totters unsteadily as though spun about by that dust storm. To a clown, they all turn away from him, wheezing with laughter, paralyzed, pulverized, unable to stand that sweet stupid grin. Clowns pinch each other, slap one another, some hold pictures of their dead relatives brought especially for such an instance, to sadden them into mere euphoria.

Thirty seconds, someone calls and the sea of clowns divides. They dive for props and wigs while someone swings the curtain wide.

They scatter to the entrance, yanking up their baggy pants, joking with each other while they gather in a clump.

The professor from State, looking on while they wait, asks,

Everybody's going out, what about Stump?

Please, gentlemen, there is a circus going on out there. Someone, anyone, have the sense to close the curtain while you double over. Thank you. You may proceed.

You heard the man, fellas. Whaddaya say? How's about Stump does a public display?

You can flush that crap right down the tubes. It's us is paying him, not them rubes.

Aw, g'wan, forget it. Don't be a jerk. Let's let the Doctor see him work.

Hat and cane! Hat and cane! Solo, Stumpy!

The curtain parts. The music starts. His props are jammed into his hands. He shrugs, resigned, and like a blind man, taps his cane out toward the stands. Like a wine bottle emptied with one last attempted snoot. Bag man, rag man, muscles gone sag man, out goes Stumpy to entertain the troops.

Down the stretch of hippodrome, Stumpy struts in all alone, cane swinging smartly to the rhythm of his trot. Stupid grin upon his face, the tiny man with snail's pace seems to grow to fill the space. Centre ring. Single spot.

He tosses his cane upwards with a slow deliberate spin; he grabs his hat and throws it, too. The cane lands balanced on his chin; the hat nestles softly on the top end of the stick. The crowd applauds him loudly at completion of the trick. Startled by the noise, Stumpy panics, loses poise and twists his neck to check upon the sources of the sound. The hat and cane both plummet off his chin and toward the ground. But wait, the cane has landed balanced on his foot instead; the hat's rotated once and landed squarely on his head. As though he knows it's futile that he ever learn its cause, Stumpy shrugs, surrenders, and accepts the crowd's applause.

He thinks for a second of another trick to do and reaches out to grab the cane that's perched upon his shoe. But somehow when he reaches, the cane's no longer there. It's to his right, he grabs again, again he's grasping air. As though it were alive, the cane dances, dodges, dives, and even seems to sneer at Stumpy's clumsy lunging stabs. It tempts him, taunts and teases, lets him come close as he pleases but manages to get away when Stumpy makes a grab. With one mighty reach, in vain, Stumpy lunges at the cane and, as he does, he stumbles, skids, and trips.

The air is full of Stump and cane and sawdust showers down like rain but Stumpy has the cane in hand when he completes the flip.

But Stumpy's problems aren't through for now the hat is on his shoe. The crowd groans loudly as it notices his plight. Stumpy shrugs, swings his foot and sends the hat in flight. The topper settles neatly high atop his brow. A tiny smirk, a braggart's wink, and Stumpy takes a bow.

With the air of a striptease, he shrugs his coat off of his sleeves and drapes it over top the cane. It's clear there's something planned. Stumpy nods his head just slightly. Down his arm the hat glides lightly; with a flip it rotates and lands gently in his hand. He lifts the cane up once again and balances it on his chin. He throws the hat. It seems to float and softly settles on his coat. Stumpy wiggles in anticipation, hitches up his baggy pants. The crowd looks on in fascination as Stumpy sets and takes his stance. Now, at last, they understand the cane will fall into his hands, the hat upon his head and the coat upon his back. Crowd and Stumpy draw a breath; the air is silent, still as death, and, at that fateful moment, the centre ring goes black.

The spotlight has gone out.

From backstage there's a shout.

My god! *it's Dr. Whatsisname from State.*

As though trapped in a bad dream that goes on despite their screams, the audience can merely sit and wait.

The lights go on, the music blares. There stands Stumpy. The crowd just stares. His cane has dropped, his hat lies crushed and propped up on his jacket that is crumpled in the dust. Stumpy picks his things up and begins the slow walk back, fading into nothing as he's passed along the track by a sequined troupe of aerialists heading for finale.

Through the curtain stumbles Stumpy, back into the alley.

Amid the trunks the old clown ambles, make-up wrecked, his clothes in shambles, backs turn toward him as he passes by. No one dares to face him should their witnessing disgrace him as if pain and pity were an issue of the eye.

The professor reaches out for Stumpy but a hand restrains his touch.

Time,

says a voice.

And time again.

That was heartless,

says the Prof.

Our lot,

chorus voices.

But to be so callous. . .

We're a thick-skinned lot.

You mean this happens all the time?

Reaching epidermic proportions.

But it's my fault,

cries the good doctor.

Why didn't you stop me?

Shhh,

the voices murmur.

Watch,

the voices purr.

Expectantly they wait for whatever to occur.

From the back end of the alley, home to Stumpy's slapstick schemes, comes a tape-recorded melody, East Indian in theme. Homemade flood-lights. Taped applause. Stumpy steps out draped in gauze, a turban on his head, a white cloth diaper 'round his rump, carrying a basket that he sets down with a thump. He steps behind the prop box and emerges with a flute, experimentally blows on it, evokes a paltry toot. Stumpy, though, seems satisfied and puts the flute down by his side. He seats himself and, painfully, assumes the lotus pose. With the tape, he plays along, a tortuous strain of snake-charm song, then glares in anger at the basket from which nothing grows. He gets up, goes behind the prop box. Clatter, crash. Out Stumpy walks clutching a dilapidated, battered old trombone. He sits himself down once again and when the taped refrain begins, he plays along in lovely, furry tones. Nothing. Not a stirring yet there's something odd occurring. Stumpy seeks the source of this odd elusive feeling. One hand above his head has found his turban has somehow come unwound and the filament of gauze rises slowly toward the ceiling. The basket remains unperturbed. Stumpy stands, now quite unnerved. Into the open lid he blares the melody with violence. From within there is a stirring, rustling noises, sounds of whirring. A sign arises from the basket reading simply "Silence!"

Stumpy's clearly come unstrung. He makes a savage headlong lunge into the basket and he grabs the rope with rage. He struggles with the strand, wraps it firmly round his hand, yanks it from the basket and half across the stage. He's won!

But as he celebrates, the rope starts to retaliate pulling Stumpy head-long into the open basket. Stumpy is trapped there upside down. Legs wave airborne as the clown struggles hard to free himself from his wicker casket. Stumpy battles his way free and lifts his arms triumphantly flourishing the limp rope coiled in a tangled heap. He flings it on the ground, stamps on it, bends down and puts his ear above it as though checking for a heartbeat. Stump at last is satisfied the hated coil of rope has died. He flings it 'cross his shoulders with a gesture of disdain. Mustering his self-respect, the dead rope wound around his neck, Stumpy gathers props while the music starts again. But wait, the rope's alive! It twists and sinuously writhes. Twining against clawing fingers, deadly and relentless, the rope snakes skyward *with its prize, the sorcerer's apprentice. Enchanter trapped by his enchantment, hoist upon his own petard, the noose about his neck tightens, cinches firmly, yanks him hard. Blackout.*

Titters, laughs, guffaws. A shout of "Bravo!" Wild applause.

Is everyone here mad?

says Doc.

Hoots. Catcalls. One-liners hopscotch disembodied in the darkened crowd.

Surely,

cries the good Professor,

you can't mean to applaud suicide?

It wasn't our applause killed him—he died by his own hand.

And don't call me Shirley.

A clown's clown,

someone says.

Bust your gut, break your ribs, crush your heart like a Christmas toy.

(for Mark Anthony)

The Story

Frank had a dynamite story. Monica was telling him, "Frank, tell Al the story. Al, you sticking with rye? Frank, honey, let me get you another." She kind of waves at us with her hand and all those pink bracelets jangle. Pink bracelets, pink nails, pink lipstick, and shiny pink pants that are stuffed just right.

Monica is something.

Frank and Monica were drinking martinis. Frank used to be a rye drinker. We'd sit out on his deck drinking ryes past sundown, talking love and oil prices—always bad news—two subjects we could go on and on about without ever having much to do with either. Or we'd end up just drinking and not saying much of anything and feeling fine about that too. But May around here in Calgary the wind can kick up something awful, so this time we were all inside.

Frank met Monica on a singles cruise last February. She wasn't quite single at the time, just separated from her second husband. Frank was taking my advice. His scrap metal business had just about stopped dead for the winter, though he had plenty of dough stashed away from the past couple of boom years. So I told him to take the cruise. That was where Patti and I met, on a cruise. Frank was wearing a Calgary Olympics pin through the heart of the alligator on his shirt and Monica asked him if he'd been there, so Frank told her he lived there, and suddenly look who couldn't look a lady in the eye his whole life and is now strolling moonlit decks with a blonde, bikinied bombshell. She was running away from Red Deer, Monica told Frank, from Barney, her first husband's ex-best friend, but who knows, she told Frank, they're probably buddy-buddy again, swapping whore-Monica jokes together at some pissant minor league hockey game. As for Frank, he was just running away from being Frank, Monica had been telling me, and just maybe he got away clean, she says. Then she takes our drink orders and says for us to sit tight.

"Some girl, eh?" says Frank. "Ever think I'd marry a girl like Monica?"

"Hell, Frank," I tell him. "Who'da ever thought anybody'd ever marry you?"

"That's right," says Frank. "But it's amazing the change in me. Hey, you notice I dropped about fifteen pounds?"

Frank was in deep. Frank was in over his head. Frank didn't know sharks in the water when they bit him and Monica bit. Me, I been swimming with them a long time. It's wives like Monica got me where I am today. It's the business. You go door-to-door selling home improvements and you get to know these women. You learn to look around and find the little things they do to fix up the house. Then you tell them how great it is, what an artistic streak they have, how their husbands must love what they did to the place. And of course, that's the key. You learn to pick the things that nobody, least of all a husband, would notice. A little conversation, a little suggestion here and there, a little fake blush when you let them catch you looking them over and suddenly you're into their dreams and they got their names on a contract. Then comes the hard part—when you got to sit down man-to-man and explain to the hubby what all this does for him. It's best to act a little swish with them. You sell dreams coming true to the women, interior decorating to the men. And sometimes, over coffee in the kitchen, the wife would reach over and I'd feel a squeeze on my knee and the invitation. It's dreams, TV dreams.

So I say, "Well, Frank. This is it, eh? It doesn't bother you, those other husbands?"

"Hell, Al," says Frank, "I think it's better this way, you know? She's had those other guys to compare me to and, hey, she still wants me."

Monica comes back in with the drinks and the martini pitcher on a tray. "My ears are bur-ning," she sings. She looks over at Frank and cocks her head, smiling. Then over at me and clucks her tongue. "Now what's he been saying about me?"

Frank looks up like an eager pet, big round-eyed stupid puppy smile. "Just telling Al how perfect you are," Frank says.

Monica walks over and bends from the waist, offering me my drink like a cocktail waitress. "Al's a little worried about me, isn't he?" she says, looking at me good and proper.

"Al's a good friend, honey," Frank says.

"That's what I meant, Frank." Then she looks away from me. "You worried, baby?"

"Do I look worried?" says Frank, looking worried.

Monica gets rid of the tray and swivels into the barcalounger, pops it back, and gets her legs crossed on the footpads. Pink toenails, too. "Al, look at that man," she says. "Frank, you've got nothing to worry about, honey," she says.

Newlyweds.

I used to do that stuff for Patti. We were married twenty-seven months.

"So come on, Frank," Monica says. "Tell Al the story."

Frank says, "Al doesn't want to hear that story."

"Sure, I do," I say.

Monica pops the barcalounger upright and hunches forward staring at Frank like he's on TV.

"Okay, okay," says Frank. "See, Al, I was downtown last Friday, and I'm stopped at a light and I see a guy walking and wearing long johns and one of those old leather pilot hats with goggles and this big towel he's got tied around his neck for a cape."

"And army boots. Don't forget the army boots," says Monica.

"Right," says Frank, "I almost forgot. And army boots. So, anyway, he's going along real slow with these real long steps and I can see he must be measuring something off. So finally he stops and turns around and he stands there like he's praying for something and then he starts to run. Then he really starts flapping his arms and then I see him like stick his arms way out and jump. My God, he's laying flat out in the air and I swear he must have been four, five feet off the ground and that's the way he hits—flat out, right on his face, wham. Oh, man, what a sight. It's like the guy never even considers that maybe he wouldn't fly."

Monica says to me, "Don't you think that's the craziest thing you ever heard?"

I see Frank just sitting there shaking his head.

So I say, "So what happened next?"

Monica says, "Listen, I'm crazy too. Like I once bought a new pair of shoes at an Eaton's sale and I wear them twice to go dancing. Second time out, both heels break. Both! So I take them back and the customer service says to me I abused them and won't give me my money back. Fucking abused them! Going dancing? So finally, they got to call the store manager over because now I'm stretched out over across the service desk pretending to be asleep so's no other customer can get any service until they finish up taking care of me. And, honey," Monica says, "I got my money back, and that's the way I am, you know?"

We sit there for awhile, just drinking. Then I reach over to put my glass down on the coffee table, which is over on the other side of the barcalounger, and Monica says, "Frank, honey, your buddy's putting the squeeze on my knee-ee."

And Frank says, "There's nobody else in the world I'd trust to squeeze your knee."

"You trust this old dog?" Monica says and she winks. "He's a fucking door-to-door salesman."

"Not Al," Frank says.

Monica throws back her head, shaking her blonde hair and sort of laughing like that was the funniest thing she ever heard.

But I see Frank look out the window, where the sun is streaming in over the deck. He says, "Just for one second I think I thought the guy might really do it."

We sit there for a while, not saying much, watching the sun go down until I lie and say, "I got dinner cooking over at my place and if I don't hurry it'll burn."

I get my jacket. I go out the back way to cut down the alley to my place. I'm in a big hurry to get home. I don't know why. I even start running and taking these big high dumb steps.

Goofy.

What the
Weej Wants

The Weej says, "You want to know what's gonna happen?"

He's already seen this one. So have I but I'm not telling The Weej. Then what would I do? *Rain Man*, then, because my parents didn't want to ask us and have The Weej say "*Friday The 13th, Part One Zillion*," or whatever it's at. And me, "I don't care." It kills my folks every time I say it. This is the kind of jerk I am. I know what it does to them when I say it but I say it.

Tom Cruise is going to the reading of his millionaire father's will. He's going to get rose bushes and an old car, and his brother's getting the rest. His nutcake brother. And his girlfriend's driving him crazy because he won't talk to her.

"Didn't you see it? I know you saw it, Eddie." He can't stand it that I might not know what happens. "C'mon, you musta saw it," says The Weej.

"Must have seen it."

"Must have seen it." Real quiet.

The Weej would never take that from his Mom. He'd say something smart. She'd quote him Scripture and then he'd say it again and again and his old lady would cry. And when his old man came home he'd get it hard across that smart mouth of his. Just the way his mouth looks makes people want to smack him, like a little *O*, like The Weej is always laughing at something. And then he'd probably open it up and do something stupid like start whispering again.

He hasn't got hit lately though. All you have to do is look out the window and you can see The Weej's bedroom from ours. Mine.

I never used to bother. The only thing you'd ever see is The Weej doing homework or him and Charlie laughing about their stupid kid secrets. Then they'd see me looking and close the curtains.

They know The Weej listens to me so I always had to babysit him and my little brother Charlie on Thursdays. This is the first Thursday I've babysat in four months. Since Charlie killed himself. Without Charlie around to tell him what to do, The Weej is worse than ever. He sits there waiting like he thinks I'm God.

"Let's do something we both can do, Eddie," he says. I know what he wants to do.

Thursday is Bible study night for Mrs. Cooper and bowling night for Mr. Cooper and my Dad. My Dad hates bowling and goes because he thinks he's supposed to like it. Thursday was bridge night for Mom with her friends but tonight she's going with Mrs. Cooper. I don't think she's becoming one of those Jesus ladies. She just can't face her friends.

I know the feeling. You go to school and the first day back everyone is different. They think it's you. And you can't do anything the way you used to, like being Evereddie, the spark plug coming off the bench in B-ball. Even if you had everything pumping just excellent it wouldn't look right to them to be doing it like nothing happened to your little brother. Even the lame stuff like slamming into lockers pretending you fainted when Jennifer Simpson walks by. And the amazing thing is Jennifer Simpson doesn't walk by, but comes up to you and says she's sorry.

Everybody's sorry.

Except when you do finally sneak off into the bathroom for one second by yourself during Bio when nobody should ever be there you hear Schmitz saying to someone in the stall, "You know why Evereddie's Mom uses Wisk on their shirts?"

The Weej has got his schoolbag on my Dad's desk and he's digging inside it pretending he's looking for his homework. I know he's done it already. He always does his homework first thing when he gets home. When it comes to school he's perfect. Most kids leave home looking exactly like their Moms and Dads want them to. Then, on the bus, they're ripping open their shirts and messing up their hair and girls are smearing on the make-up while The Weej is tucking in his shirt and working away at that black mop of his with a comb.

"Whatever you want to do is all right with me," he says. "I brought something for us to do in case you're bored with the movie." He fiddles in the bag and I know he's rubbing the board. The Weej and his Ouija board. He sleeps with it. "You can tell me what you want to know. Really." Like this is something he thinks I've been waiting forever to hear.

He made it in shop class. He almost flunked because he was supposed to finish three woodworking projects—a letter-opener, a candy dish shaped like the state, and then a free choice—but all he got done was the board. Technically he should have flunked but he got a prize for it in the Board of Ed craft fair. So they couldn't flunk him. He'd just turned thirteen. Nobody called him Lester after that. You can bet how thrilled his Mom was.

The thing about it was it didn't work. He and Charlie started messing with it but nothing would happen. No messages, just alphabet soup. Or if something did happen they'd argue and Charlie would start screaming that The Weej was pushing the little pointer table. Which is when I had to tell them to shut up or I'd break the stupid thing. But what happened is The Weej would start whining until I ended up having to do it with them. The very first time, I just put my hand on it and the pointer table started to go. I didn't push it, I didn't even look at it and the little table started floating across the bottom board pointing to the letters and numbers.

It was stupid. First of all, I guess since it was his Ouija board it only answered The Weej's questions, never Charlie's or mine even if we were the two guys touching the pointer. And second, we never knew if it was answering any questions at all. The Weej would never tell us what he was asking. He said he couldn't tell us before the answer came in or it wouldn't work. And forget about having him ask a question you really wanted answered. Oh, he'd try to figure out what he thought Charlie wanted. Charlie would sit there staring at him like he was trying to drill the questions into that big hollow head but The Weej hardly ever guessed right. Like the pointer would touch the NO and then The Weej would brush at the little fuzz on his lip and say, "Charlie can forget about shaving for the rest of this year." Something stupid like that. And Charlie would sit there staring right through The Weej like there was something else he was looking at.

So it wouldn't work even if I told him what to ask. Charlie's dead and there's only me so The Weej is desperate. The Weej will do anything so I won't hate him.

He's looking over at me sideways waiting for me to give up on the movie. I can see his reflection off the screen but I'm watching Tom Cruise trying to weasel his way into that house because his brother has got to watch *People's Court.* Dustin Hoffman's driving him crazy. The same thing over and over and over can drive you crazy. I'm waiting for the part where all the toothpicks fall on the ground and Dustin Hoffman's going to figure out right away how many there are.

I know he's supposed to be kind of a genius and kind of an idiot and I know it's only a movie but I don't see how he can do it. Different brains, I guess. We've all got different brains.

Take Charlie's brain. The way I always saw it was like the crown on the Statue of Liberty—all these little ideas that stuck out in different directions. He'd never get very far with any of them. The Weej is the exact opposite. He gets stuck on one idea and twists it every which way. It's like a firehose, snaking around in every direction with no fireman to hold onto it. I've got a brain shaped like a regular old brain—everything goes in from the back, swirls around until it's all sorted out, then slips on out the way it came and then I know what to do. Except some of it just never comes back out.

The way someone can see everything without trying. I don't get it.

The Weej takes out the board and the pointer, rattling it so I can hear. He's sitting there with his fingers on the pointer waiting and I know nothing's happening.

They had me go see a shrink. I only went the one time. I hated having him watching me. I'm not the one needs watching. They told me he was supposed to help me figure things out. Okay, I told him, figure this out. What I was doing was having the most excellent day of my basketball life, scoring seventeen, six assists, two steals, and four rebounds against Central High while Charlie was hanging himself in our garage.

I'm the sixth man. When I'm not playing I keep my mouth shut and watch and when the starting five come to the bench on a time-out I tell them what kind of defence the other team's playing on them. Then I slap them on the back and tell them how great they are and to go out there and kill 'em. Usually I see a lot of action but I don't expect to this year in the Central game even though Schmitz has three offensive fouls in the first seven minutes. Coach Trebelhorn is swearing to himself, "Don't that stupid S.O.B. see what they're doing to him?" So I say, "It's a Diamond-One and they're sagging on him in the paint." He looks over at me with his jaw hanging like I'm some kind of Einstein and that's when Schmitz tries to elbow his way through three guys and picks up his third foul. Coach T sends me in. I think I hear everybody groan. But this year I am Evereddie, all right. I got my shoes pumped, and I can see everything—where the lanes open up and where they back off from me on the perimeter. The ball slaps into my hands and snaps out and there's a charge that runs right through me and out my fingertips. I hit my first four shots—three three-pointers and a give-and-go from Nelson that I sink with two Central guys all over me.

Central calls time out to freeze me at the foul line and I look up to the stands for Charlie, thinking, this is how you're supposed to do it, Lamebrain. My Dad is jumping up and down like an idiot and Mom practically has tears in her eyes and there's no Charlie. I look for him kneeling at courtside with his camera. No Charlie. This is impossible, I'm thinking. They bring Charlie to every game. He's got pictures of me in every game I've played. Charlie's in the bathroom, or Charlie is sitting with The Weej in the Lame Seats, or he's under the stands reloading film in his camera. I don't think about it the rest of the game because I play every minute and we squeak by in the last five seconds on Nelson's free throws.

Everybody's pounding me and Nelson on the back and my Dad fights his way through and gives me a bear hug and swings me up off the ground and someone from the paper takes a shot of us. It's only after I'm showered and changed I ask them. Mom says, "Your brother is almost fourteen and if he says he's got a science project due I'm not making him come to a basketball game. But I'm certainly glad I didn't stay home with him. I wouldn't have missed this for the world, Edward." She hugs me and Dad hugs us both. Then we go home and Dad hits the garage door opener and we see him just hanging from a rafter.

His face was black.

Last week, the guy from the school paper sent us a copy of the picture he took of Dad and me. Of course they didn't use it. No note or anything, just the picture. I'm sure he didn't mean anything by it but Dad started crying and tore it up. Then he saw me watching and said how sorry he was and what I was supposed to say was that it was okay. I probably would have torn it up myself. But what I do is shrug my shoulders and go upstairs to my room. That's the kind of jerk I am.

They're dancing in the Las Vegas hotel room. Tom Cruise is teaching him because Dustin Hoffman thinks he's got to know how to dance on a date with a hooker. The date's never going to happen.

I hear this little noise behind me. The Weej is sitting at the desk with his head in his hands.

I see him like this at his house, sometimes. I shouldn't spy on him but I can't help it. When I'm sitting at my desk my window looks right out on his bedroom.

I have to say something.

"You want a Coke?" I say.

"You hate me," he says. I don't answer. I'm thinking of his stupid mouth, the way it looked when his parents came over the next day. Not surprised, not anything different. The same stupid mouth. Like he was laughing at something.

"I don't hate you," I say finally.

"You think I knew he was gonna do it, don't you?"

I'm the one that should have known. That's what I'm thinking. How can you live in the same house, sleep in the same room all the time with the same person and not know? How can you look at Charlie and The Weej every day and not see what's going on? That means you might be missing everything. Anything can happen. When I think that, I can feel it like the whole weight of the air crushing me. You can't watch everything all the time.

I don't know what to say. So I say, "I'm going to get a Coke." The Weej is not even looking at me. He's staring down at his hands on the board.

I go to the kitchen. I'm closing the fridge when I hear this crash. I don't want to be here.

He's knocked the board off the desk and now he's flat out crying. I'm standing there stupid with Coke foam dripping off my hand onto the rug. I should do something but I don't want to touch him.

The Weej buries his face again. He's moaning, "I was supposed to be the one."

I know what he's going to say and I don't want to hear it. I could just walk away but I don't. I'm thinking about last year's final. Knowing what's coming all along and still having to see it. Central scored to go ahead with two seconds left. We called time and Coach T sketched it all out. Schmitz set a perfect screen, Nelson hit me with a bullet inbounding pass. I turned from behind the three-point line, completely unguarded, and shot with the buzzer going off. There was no chance. I knew that. No chance at all but I couldn't stop watching the ball coming down, knowing it was already over. When it hit off the front rim everybody else was dying. But I already knew. I just made myself watch it.

He says, "Me. It was always me. It should've been me."

I'm thinking, yes, it should have. But I can't say that.

Then he says, "What am I gonna do?"

He's waiting for an answer.

What I say is, "Pick it up." I say it mean.

The Weej lifts his head up and looks over surprised. I see his stupid mouth get bigger and rounder and I say, "Pick it up," again real loud. He gets up slow, staring at me, and picks up the board and the pointer and he's standing there like he doesn't know what to do with it.

"Put it down on the desk." The Weej is like a yelled-at dog slinking away like I might hit him. I don't care.

I yell, "Put it down! Sit down!"

He sets the board and pointer table back on the desk and slumps back down in the desk chair. I pull up across the desk from him in Mom's swivel chair. "You aren't going to do anything, got it?"

The Weej nods slow at me.

I say, "Listen to me!"

He knows I know.

I say, "You owe me."

His mouth stretches wide across the bottom, quivering the more he tries to hold it all in. Then he goes nuts. He starts hitting himself in the face over and over.

"Stop it!" I yell. But he just keeps slapping. I grab his hands and squeeze. "Don't do that. You hear me?"

The way he looks at me.

"It's not your fault." He makes me say that.

He nods and I wait until his hands go weak. I let go and he puts them back down on the pointer table. He sits there staring down. I feel like if I look at him now I'm going to have to look at him for the rest of my life.

Tom Cruise is yelling at Dustin Hoffman. The movie's almost over. He's got to let his brother go back to the nuthouse. Dustin Hoffman's on the train and he just kind of disappears inside without even saying goodbye. Tom Cruise is calling him back to tell him something but when he comes back there's really nothing to say.

"Eddie?"

I look over at him and The Weej says, "What's gonna happen?"

I'm thinking about it again, how anything can happen. I can barely move. "I don't know," I say.

Then he reaches out and takes my hands and he stretches them out and down on the pointer like he's plugging them in. When he puts his hands back down on his side I can feel the little table start to move, floating across the letters, pointing out the future.

Cab Ride

Airport? I'll stow the rest of the bags. Hey, no, sit up with me, man. Lemme tell you a story.

Cabbies always got to hear stories so for once I want to talk. I got a right. They say shrinks, barbers, and bartenders hear every story ever told. You think that makes them experts on human nature? No. Guy'll walk out of his shrink's office middle of a gorgeous spring day pull out a handgun, boom, blow away some total stranger, and the shrink, what's he gonna say? He don't know this guy's gonna do this? Hell of an advertisement. No. He says, and this I believe, he says, of course we all have the *capacity* for violence but. . . . But, but, but. That guy puts a finger on the door handle of this cab, I know. Hell, I've got the Not For Hire sign going up the moment I see a guy like that. Barbers? They don't know. You go to any barber. You sit down and practically draw the man blueprints for a haircut and still when he spins you around you look like Boris Karloff. They don't know.

And bartenders. That's what I was getting to. This was about four months ago. No, no, let me think. It was December 23. That was Friday before Christmas about 10 P.M. and it was hell. Temperature had dropped about twenty degrees since sundown and it was starting to snow.

I pick up this fare at the airport. First thing I notice—no bags. No carry on, nothing. Second thing, he's wearing what's gotta be a five hundred dollar suit but it's beat. I mean this suit is not one of your linen L.A. jobs, this suit's wool blend, double-breasted, fits the man like a glove but stained like he took it swimming in a bowl of soup. And the man inside the suit. You see Gary Cooper in that movie, something, something John Doe? Where he's a guy down and out and gets famous then gets to be a nobody again? Only to me he always looks like Gary Cooper wearing a bum suit. Well, this is that guy. It wasn't like he was dangerous—just wrung out.

So I pick the guy up and he says, "Downtown." I say, "You want to be little more specific? Downtown's a pretty big place." And then I start telling him how I got here and how the economy shut down all the plants which is why I drive cab. He looks at me a second then reaches in his inside jacket pocket and pulls out a wad of bills. No wallet, just bills, a fistful all crumpled up and he peels off two tens and says, "Here's twenty bucks. Just drive. Don't talk. When we get downtown I'll tell you." I shrug and shut up. Hey, twenty bucks. There's no way I have twenty bucks worth of stuff to say to this guy, right? The guy buries his face in his hands and hunches down in the back seat so all I can see in the rear view is his fifty dollar haircut.

I take the expressway down to Riverside and turn right, alongside the river, and I'm thinking twenty bucks or no, I got to ask this guy where he wants me to cross or we'll pass downtown altogether and I'm just about to say something when he lifts up and says "Fourth Street Bridge." I'm just about two blocks away. I go down, make the turn. The guy is now sitting way forward, looking out the front windshield through the snow and the wiper slush. He's got his head almost on my right shoulder and he yells "Stop!" We're in the middle of the bridge so I figure he means the other side but he yells, "Stop right now, damn it!" I say, "I can't stop here. We're in the middle of the goddamn bridge." And the guy goes nuts, reaching over trying to grab the wheel and shit. Well, I smack him one backhand with my right hand like this? I hit him smack in the face and the guy just collapses. I think, oh shit, this is it. This suit is some influential bastard, some lawyer who's just been out drinking for two days and I smacked him. He's gonna sue my ass, sue my company's ass, sue my mother's grave's ass. I pull over on the other side of the bridge and he's just sitting there, face in his hands.

"Jeez, I'm sorry," I say. "I thought you were gonna kill us both back there. I can't stop in the middle of a bridge, you know. It's illegal. Hey, you okay?" I ask him 'cause he just stays there hunched over and I know I didn't hit him that hard. But he don't say a thing. So I ask him, "You got some place to go?" and he don't look up, just shakes his head. "Let me take you some place." But he don't move, he don't talk, he don't do nothing. "Look," I say, "I can't leave you here. It's snowing like a bastard and it's minus twenty out there. You don't have no coat. Let me take you to a nice place I know. You can have a drink and pull yourself together, okay?" And I just pull out, heading for Charlie's Fireside. You know Charlie's? It's a nice place. Beautiful old bar, nice people, dark, so's the stains on his suit aren't going to look too bad.

So I drive him down to Charlie's and stop. The guy looks up. Man, he is pitiful so I say, "This one's on me," and hand him back his tens. The guy says, "No, no, you keep it. Here," and hands me another ten. By now I don't want another thing to do with this guy so I take the bill. Then the dispatcher cuts in and has a call for a cab down on the Strip just a couple blocks south and west. I respond and I'm about to pull out but I just wait and make sure this guy gets in to Charlie's all right. I watch until the big wood door closes behind him and take the call over the Strip. Three college boys are too plastered. I take them back to the U but I just can't get this airport fare off my mind. So I go off duty for ten and drive back to Charlie's. I go in and tell the bartender there about this fare I dropped off and ask if he's seen him and the bartender jerks his thumb down the end of the bar and there's my fare drinking and staring into the mirror. I tell the bartender, "Look, I don't know what's with this guy but see he's all right." The bartender says to me, "What do I look like, a fucking babysitter?" So I hand him two of the guy's tens and talk to him hard. "Make sure this guy gets himself a cab and some place to go, got it?" He takes the bills and says, "It's your money." I go back to the cab and run a couple of people from one bar to another. I end up way the hell out the west side and the dispatcher starts bitching I'm supposed to be working the airport which is true only everytime I drop off a fare, I've been round the corner from the next call.

Anyway, I head east on Riverside and I'm there again, at the Fourth Street Bridge. There's cop cars, ambulances, lights flashing everywhere. I pull over and come running out, slipping in the snow and they're laying out my fare. Drowned and near froze solid. I grab a couple of cops and tell them I know the guy and they take me over inside a cop car and I tell them everything. All they want to know is do I know the guy's name and I say no. I ask them are they going down to Charlie's and they say sure, in a couple of minutes. I get back in my cab and the dispatcher's screaming at me. I know I should be heading back to the airport but I go to Charlie's Fireside. The bartender's just saying last call. I don't know what it was about the guy but I hated his guts. I tell him my fare's dead, the one he was supposed to watch out for. "What do I care?" he says. I grab a fistful of his shirt and tell him he damn well better care. I tell him there's a guy croaked himself after drinking at his bar and the cops want to talk to him. He's not cracking so wise now. He's dribbling and babbling he did what I said, he got the guy a cab, what do I want from him. The cab company, I say. He don't know the cab company, and squeezing his neck don't make him remember. Then the cops come in and pull me off him. What did I tell you about bartenders, all the stories they hear? They don't know. I spend the rest of the night in the slammer.

So that's it. I spent a couple months trying to track down the cabbie. You'd think one driver ought to be able to find another. I didn't find shit. Don't even know what company. What the hell kind of cabbie drops a drunk off, middle of a snowstorm, no coat, halfway across a bridge? Here we are. Just a second. What's your hurry? I'll get your bags.

You know what I think? I think the guy had it all planned out. Maybe last time he was in town his business wasn't going so good or his wife is cheating on him. Maybe he knows this. He sees the bridge and this was in his mind. Like this is some place to jump from. Say then he loses his job, his wife walks out. He could lay down some cash, take a plane, get in a cab, get out and jump. Nobody'd be the wiser. Just him. This is what I think. A guy like that, this could be you. He could have parents still alive, maybe some kids he loves. He don't want them to know he's killing himself. Better to just go missing. Nobody knows for sure. Nobody blames themselves.

Only there's me. The guy doesn't figure on me. I start to talk to him the way I do when somebody interesting gets in my cab. And this gets to him. But then for twenty bucks I shut up. So what do I really care, he figures. Say I don't take the twenty bucks, he and I get to talking. I tell him my story, he tells me his. Things don't look so bad. Maybe I put the Not For Hire sign up a half-hour or so and sit down with him at Charlie's. Maybe we end up back at the airport and he's heading home for Christmas somewhere. He don't deserve to end up frozen dead in a five hundred dollar suit. There you go. You want a porter?

This's been driving me nuts four months now. I mean it's like every time somebody gets in the cab I think, "How's this guy doing? He okay?" He's in my cab but he don't even think about me. People think their life is like a story. They want to end it, boom, story over. It don't work that way. You live, you start a million different stories and all the people you meet are in them. You die and the stories and the rest of us go on, just no ending.

(for I.M.P.)